SEEKING THE SHERIFF

MASTERSON COUNTY BOOK 1

CALLE J. BROOKES

SEEKING THE SHERIFF

For information contact:

www.callejbrookes.com

Book and Cover design by C.J. BROOKES

First Edition: MAY2017

REED: 06052020

10 9 8 7 6 5 4 3 2 1

1

SHERIFF JOEL MASTERSON WANTED TO KICK the kid's ass seven ways to Sunday, but he controlled himself. Barely. The boy was too old for this stupid shit.

Joel was, that was for sure. He grabbed Phoenix Tyler by the back of his collar and dragged him to his feet. "Come on. I haven't got all night."

Tyler protested, curses ringing out through the night. Main Street was fully deserted except for him, Tyler, and the man twice the kid's size who he'd started the fight with.

The two wannabe wrestlers smelled like the whiskey distillery on the outskirts of town, and

Joel's eyes burned from the strength of it. But his hands were steady on the kid.

Best to get Tyler out of there before Rutherford got the idea to give the kid the beating Tyler most likely deserved.

Rutherford wasn't known for Friday night barroom brawls.

Neither was Tyler, for that matter. Now, underage drinking...well, Deputy Lowell had picked him up for that a time or two already, hadn't he?

Nothing Joel hadn't seen a hundred times in his two years as the sheriff of Masterson County.

Time to return this boy to where he belonged, so Joel and the deputies could get out around the county. They needed to make certain the floods that were impending hadn't washed out the access roads. Five thousand people resided in the county, and if too many roads were flooded out, the entire county would be impacted.

He didn't have time for some punk wannabe with a chip on his shoulder right now. The floods headed their way were supposed to be record breaking. And he didn't know if the dams were going to be strong enough to keep the waters at bay.

It was going to get bad in Masterson County, Wyoming— really bad.

And it was his job to keep the people in his county safe. It wasn't a responsibility he took lightly.

He cuffed the Tyler kid and shoved him in the back of his SUV, thankful for the metal grill that separated Tyler from his seat. It took a call to his dispatcher to find out where the boy lived—while he'd had a few brushes with the law, Joel hadn't dealt with him personally before—and then he headed his SUV toward the far southwestern corner of his county. As he covered the familiar territory, he wondered about the kid in his back seat. There were a bunch of Tylers out past his family homestead, but he'd never met all of them.

The boy was one of *those* Tylers, then. They'd been contentious sonsofbitches since before the county was formed. He'd had more than a few run-ins with the boy's uncles and cousins.

Looks like Phoenix Tyler was following the family footsteps right down a bad path.

Joel sighed, wishing the world he lived in could be a hell of a lot different. Part of the problem with the Tylers *he* knew was a simple lack of economic opportunity. They were ranchers, pure and simple, and in Tyler Township, where they lived, the lands were barren and inhospitable. Nothing worth a damn would grow there, and nothing could *live* there.

Except for ornery Tylers, that was. Despite the odds, the Tylers kept on.

He'd been to this corner of the county numerous times, but not to the particular address he was headed toward now.

The kid continued to mouth off in the back of the SUV. Joel just kept driving. It wasn't the first time a dumb kid took a ride home in his SUV. At least this one wasn't puking everywhere.

It was a forty-minute drive from Masterson to the Tyler ranch. The kid ended up snoring in the back before they were halfway there.

Maybe he'd sleep off most of it and be able to deal with his parents then?

Parents were sometimes the hardest part of his job. Especially parents of screwups like the boy drooling in his back seat.

He reached the Tyler ranch and turned down the pitted and rutted lane. They needed about four loads of gravel to even make it halfway passable, didn't they?

The house was sprawling but in such disrepair

on the outside that he wondered why it hadn't been condemned yet. Although it *did* look like someone had planted flowers along the walkway recently.

That saddened him more than anything. The flowers spoke of hope and a desire to at least *try*. The house screamed of neglect and despair.

He looked around one more time. He wasn't so certain he wanted to leave the boy here.

The yard was trimmed neatly and free of clutter at least. That told him a lot. *Someone*, at least, was trying.

Joel tensed when the light flicked on in the front of the house. They'd heard him pull up.

He parked next to the small porch and killed the engine. He had a feeling he was going to be there for a while. It just always seemed to happen that way at Tyler homesteads. Whether Joel wanted it to or not.

The door opened, and a middle-aged man wearing a white tank and faded jeans stepped outside. His hair was thinning and gray, and his eyes showed years of hard living, but his body was tough and lean. He looked like a hundred other weathered ranchers Joel had seen through the years. "What's wrong?"

His voice was roughened and harsh, but un-threatening. Joel cataloged the man quickly. A man just trying to get by in a world that wasn't always easy to navigate. Like so many others in Masterson County. "You Phil Tyler?"

"Yes."

"I have your boy in the back seat. Got into a brawl at Dan's Tavern in Masterson. I was going to book him in, but to be honest, I have to deal with the approaching storms. I don't have time for underage drinking, and my deputies are all spread over the county."

"He facing charges?"

Joel thought for a moment. "I'm not sure yet. Have him at my office Tuesday at ten, and we can discuss it."

He pulled the teenager from the back seat, and the kid came awake, swinging and swearing.

His father stepped off the porch and grabbed the boy by the shoulder. "Phoenix, shut your mouth before it gets you into deeper trouble."

The boy cursed his father up one side and down the other. The older man never lifted a hand to hit him, at least. If anything, the father looked more embarrassed than angry.

The kid's tirade went on for a good fifteen

minutes before the front door opened again and *six* more bodies came tumbling out.

Joel studied them quickly. Young. Three were female, small, slim, startlingly pretty in the bright porch light, and—if he wasn't mistaken—two were identical. The rest were boys, younger than the one still cursing. Hell, the youngest had to be under eight or nine, didn't he?

The rest of the Tylers?

Joel turned back to the boy when the kid started swinging. The father, no more than five nine or five ten, was a few inches shorter than his son. And a whole lot soberer.

Joel didn't have time to suffer fools gladly. Or wait for a father to gain control of his son. He grabbed the back of the kid's shirt and lifted him off his feet. While Phoenix Tyler was close to six feet tall, Joel dwarfed him. At six foot four, two hundred and fifty pounds, he was twice what the boy weighed.

He used that to his advantage now. He turned Phoenix toward him. "Get your shit together *now*. Or I will run you into town, and you can hang out in the drunk tank for the next seventy-two hours. How would you like that?"

"You can't do that. I have school tomorrow," the boy sneered.

"You could just be truant then. We'll see how well that goes over with the school." Masterson public schools had a zero-tolerance truancy policy that was strictly enforced. Every parent knew that. Jail wouldn't be an excuse.

The boy continued to kick and fight. Joel continued to hold him. He could do this all night if he had to.

2

PHOEBE TYLER SAW THE LIGHTS AND KNEW something was going on. Something that shouldn't be. She didn't even bother trying to listen, as she'd lost the ability to distinguish most sounds when she'd been six years old. She wasn't fully hearing-impaired and could speak, but there was a lot she missed. Especially without the hearing aid currently sitting on her bedside table. She'd tried to sleep with it in before, but it just didn't happen.

A fact a lot of her siblings took advantage of. Especially the younger ones. They'd better not be up wandering the house. Not this late.

She was the oldest of eight, and she didn't take that role lightly. Her father busted his butt trying to turn a profit on the small ranch that had been in their family for generations. But it wasn't easy. Especially since her mother had passed two years earlier in a car wreck that had two of her siblings injured. Leaving a mountain of debt bigger than the mountain that she could see from her window. The loss of their mother left the day-to-day care of the ranch house, and her youngest siblings, up to *her*.

Well, up to her and her sisters, Pip, Perci, and Pandora. The girls had their own responsibilities, though. Pip was doing her best to build a horse ranch out of their small stable of cutting horses. A few more years, and she'd be able to sell off some of the horses she'd bred and trained herself. Perci helped Phoebe with her Angora goat herd when needed—and worked extra twelve-hour shifts as a nurse at the county hospital whenever she could. Perci made a point of taking every bit of overtime she could get. Pan spent most of *her* time helping their father and Phoebe. When she could, Pan did virtual-assistant work and cleaned houses for some of their cousins and uncles. Phoebe's responsibilities around the house made it impossible for her to have a full-time job. She supplemented what her sisters brought in with her goats. She sold the mohair yarn she created herself. Money was tight, but they were holding on.

In her spare time, Phoebe tended her little drove. After she had finished with that, she would sit at her loom and weave blankets from the yarn she kept back for that purpose. When those sold, she'd bring in a few hundred dollars each.

Every penny their branch of the Tylers could bring in helped their family of nine survive.

If something was wrong with one of the children, it was Phoebe's job to take care of them. She didn't bother with a robe or slippers. She grabbed the hearing aid sitting on her night table and slipped it in. With the device, she had close to sixty percent of hearing in her left ear.

Phoebe hurried down the stairs.

JOEL CAUGHT THE DOOR OPENING AGAIN AS HE held the idiot teenager aloft and lectured. Another woman stepped out. He looked at her long enough to figure out if she was the mother or not. She looked like all the rest of the females but smaller, slighter. A little older. Maybe, but not much. She wore small, thin pajamas that did little to hide the fact that she was all woman. Hell, Joel would far rather be looking at *her* than dealing with this kid.

She took one look at what was happening and jumped right into the fray. By smacking at *Joel* and lecturing *him*.

Joel couldn't defend himself and the boy from the small tornado attacking him—not without seriously hurting her—so he dropped the boy heedlessly to the ground and grabbed the woman by her arms. He tried to turn her to face him more fully, but she was mighty resistant.

"Stop. Lady, I said *stop*, unless you want to be arrested for assaulting an officer."

She had one little finger pointing in his face, but she wasn't looking at him. No, now her brothers got the rest of her tirade. She had the younger ones hurrying back inside with a few sharp words, under the direction of one of the sisters. The twin females remained on the porch. Watching silently, warily.

Joel wrapped his arms around her and bear-hugged her when she waved her hands around again. He didn't have time for this. No matter that he was half enjoying having such a sweet-smelling female in his arms again. If she just wasn't trying to *kick* him with her bare little feet...

Joel lifted her straight off the ground and held her there, aloft. "*Stop*. Now."

"Don't *hurt* her, Sheriff! She can't *hear* you," the father said, hurrying closer. He reached out like he was going to try and take her out of Joel's arms. Joel wasn't about to put her down just yet. Not until she stopped kicking. "My girl is deaf. I don't think the hearing aid is on. Battery doesn't always work right."

THERE WAS A STRANGE MAN HOLDING HER. Phoebe hadn't gotten a good look at him, but she thought it was that brute, Tom Rutherford, who'd been harassing Phoenix for weeks. He certainly felt big enough to be Rutherford.

She felt his chest rumble as he spoke behind her. Felt his arms tighten around her yet again. He certainly was a large man. Strong.

Phoenix jumped to his feet and charged the cowboy holding her. The cowboy twisted. His arms tightened around her, almost protectively.

He jerked as her brother struck him on the side.

They almost went down, but the man was strong. Big and muscled...and royally ticked off.

He let go of her, and Phoebe scurried away. The man grabbed her brother. Within seconds he had Phoenix wrestled to the ground—and handcuffed. It was then that Phoebe saw the emblem on the side of the SUV.

Oh, hell. She'd just accosted the Masterson County sheriff.

Phoebe pushed Perci's helping hand away. "Get inside, with Pan and the boys. I'll deal with this."

"Phoebe, let Dad deal with it," her slightly younger sister said.

"No." She'd deal. She'd made the situation so much worse; it was her responsibility to clean it all up. Phoebe rose to her feet and turned to the man now glowering down at her. She got her first good look at the sheriff.

Even in the light from the front porch, it was hard to miss the gorgeous cowboy in jeans and a white Stetson staring at her. If he wasn't about to eat her for lunch, she would almost be tempted to stop and just stare at him.

"*You.*" He pointed right at her. Phoebe stood her ground and refused to look away.

3

He should arrest them both. Let them spend the next three days thinking about what they had done. Tempting; very, very tempting.

Thunder cracked overhead; lightning streaked across the sky. Decision made. He didn't have time for the damned Tylers of Tyler Township. Not tonight.

He looked at the woman standing so proud, defiant, and *terrified* in front of him. She was disheveled from wrestling with him, hair everywhere, and the top two buttons of the thin pajamas had popped open. He pointed at her and then the house. "Inside."

She touched her left ear lightly. "You don't have to shout. My hearing aid is turned on...now."

"March your little...*self* inside."

She obeyed, tiny chin in the air. The damned woman didn't have any shoes on. She didn't seem to notice. Her father and sisters hurried inside in front of her.

Her brother was still cursing him up one side and down the other. He cursed his sister, too. That just pissed Joel off even more. Joel yanked the kid to his feet and frog-marched him after his sister.

Damn it.

He should just arrest them both and be done with it. The old man spoke first. "Arrest my son if you need to. Let him sit for a while. But my daughter...she's needed here. She takes care of the kids. Don't think we can do it a day around here without her."

One of her sisters handed her a cotton robe, and she slipped into it quickly. She eyed him like he was a rabid rattlesnake out to gobble her up. He thought of that for a quick moment, gobbling her right up. At any other time, under any other circumstances...

He stayed silent as she tied the robe around her body.

He had to admit he liked what he'd seen in the few seconds before she covered up. He was a man, after all. None of the four women were exactly slouches in the looks department. Then she turned back toward him, and he got his first *real* look at his assailant.

Her hair was rich auburn, her eyes a soft blue. It was coloring shared with all her sisters and two of her brothers. Her skin was flawless, the body beneath the shapeless robe was small but curved. He'd had his hands on her, after all. She'd curved in all the right female places.

She stared back at him. Finally, she licked her lips nervously and spoke. "I didn't realize you were the police, Deputy..."

"*Sheriff.* I'm Joel Masterson."

She winced. "I didn't know who you were. I thought you were the men who have been harassing my brother. I am so sorry."

Such pride, it was in her face and in the way, she did not look away. He still saw the fear. Especially when she looked at the three younger boys watching from the hallway.

She made him feel like a total ass. Did she think he was going to slap some cuffs on her and drag her away, right in front of her brothers and sisters?

Damn it, one sister looked about ready to cry, as it was.

Her brother Phoenix cursed at her; she barely glanced at him, as if she were used to the treatment.

Joel wasn't. He and his three brothers had been raised never to talk to a woman like that, let alone a sister. He yanked the boy around and got in his face. "One more word out of you and it's the back of my Denali and a seventy-two-hour hold. Minimum." He sat the boy back on his feet and turned toward the oldest sister.

The woman—from her brother's curses, he assumed her name was *Phoebe*—held herself so still. She just stared at him.

Hell, Joel wanted to stare right back. He almost did. Until the boy called his sister something so foul that his father smacked him in the head.

Phil Tyler looked at Joel, resolution in his manner. "He's nineteen now and getting into more and more trouble. I got three more boys coming up right behind him. He ain't pulling his weight around here. He's just making more trouble for me —and for the girls. The four of them are working themselves to the bones around here. Just to help make ends meet. *He's* not."

Joel really didn't need the family history. What he needed was to get out of there. If the boy had been more cooperative, he'd have just left him for his father to deal with. Thanks to the sister, it had turned into an even bigger mess. "I'm sorry for your troubles, Mr. Tyler, but—"

The older man took the cup one of his twins handed him. He stared at Joel for a long moment. Like he was looking inside Joel and taking his measure somehow. It was disconcerting. Joel would admit that.

Then Phil Tyler looked at his four beautiful daughters. He straightened his shoulders, and his resolve tightened around him almost visibly.

Joel knew something significant was happening. He just didn't know what.

"I'm *asking* you to arrest him, Sheriff. Or at least get him out of here. For a while. Before he ends up hurting someone here. Every last one of my others are smaller than he is—you can see that for yourself. I just don't trust him here anymore. He's going to hurt one of them eventually."

The oldest sister protested, but her father held up a hand and told her to be quiet. She obeyed.

The entire room was silent. "He would've plowed right over you, Phoebe Kate. We all know that. Had the sheriff not been here, he could have hurt you."

"Had the *sheriff* not been *here*, it wouldn't have happened," she said, sending a glare Joel's way as if he were the cause of their family drama. Not exactly a reaction he hadn't seen in his job before. Everyone looked to blame the police. It was easier than thinking their loved one was at fault.

The brother kept cursing, though now under his breath.

"*No.* No more coddling him; our family just can't afford this any longer." The father leveled a look at the son. It was a look that was filled with love, exasperation, and disgust. "No more. You're welcome home when you can be a part of this family—*help* instead of screwing everything up. Again. Do you think we can afford bail money for this? Your sisters are struggling to find *grocery* money, Phoenix. Groceries. To feed eight other people besides *you!* You want to see Parker, Pete, or Pat go to bed hungry every night just to keep you out of jail?"

Now the kid shut up. The oldest sister moved to stand between her father, brother, and Joel. She looked up, between the two men and the boy. Joel's nose tickled, the scent of clean woman right there in front of him. She turned more fully toward her father, putting all those dark-red curls right beneath his chin. She only came up to mid-chest on him. If he leaned forward a bit, he could...

Joel forced himself to focus on doing his job and not acting like an idiot.

"Daddy—"

The older man wrapped a hand around his daughter's arm and pulled her close for a hug. He then sat her back. Closer to Joel. "*No*, baby girl. It's time he learned to be a man. Sheriff, take him off my property, please. He's not welcome here anymore."

Joel didn't see where he had a choice. The boy wasn't welcome at home any longer. He had committed a crime. And he was too drunk to be able to take care of himself. Responsibility was going to have to fall to him. Hell, he even understood where Phil Tyler was coming from. Joel reached for the boy—just as six feet of enraged drunken teenager lunged toward his father.

Knocking his five-foot one-hundred-pound sister carelessly out of his way.

Joel knew he was too late, even as he was moving.

He'd just managed to wrap one hand around her skinny little arm when she hit the floor. Her head cracked against the chair on her way down.

4

Strong arms were holding her, carrying her. For a moment, Phoebe thought she was a little girl again, held safely in her father's arms.

He had always been her safety.

And then the pain in her skull registered.

Phoebe cried out and tried to grab her skull and put it back inside her head where it belonged.

It didn't happen.

"Shhh, honey, we are at the hospital now. They will get you fixed right up. My brother's a doctor here. He'll make you feel better real soon. Just rest your head on my shoulder. I'll carry you in."

She didn't recognize the voice—and her father

hadn't been able to carry her in a really long time. Her eyes popped open, and she looked straight up —at the sheriff of Masterson County.

That's when she remembered.

Phoenix. Poor Phoenix, who'd made so many foolish decisions in the two years since they'd lost their mother in a car accident. Her brother had been driving.

And now their father had finally had enough. She'd known it was coming for a long while. Phoenix was just too far out of control. Between the troubles at school, the arguments with her father, with the twins and Pan, with the younger boys, with *her* it was just too much. The common denominator was *always* Phoenix.

She couldn't deal with this now, not with the way her head was about to explode.

"I'm pretty sure my brains are leaking out of my skull right now—" She closed her eyes again and lowered her head gingerly to the man's rock-hard shoulder. She was just going to have to stay right where she was for a little while.

5

Dr. Nathaniel Masterson was just finishing up with the last small crisis at the Masterson General Hospital when the pneumatic doors of the ER opened. His older brother walked in, arms full of woman. For a terse moment, Nate thought the small redhead was the woman he'd spent the last two hours mentally cursing. And then his attention shifted to the woman walking *behind* his brother.

There *she* was. For lack of a better definition, his personal nemesis. His albatross. There wasn't a single hospital employee that he struggled to get along with except Persephone Tyler, the last nurse hired by his predecessor. And one he'd love to fire.

If he'd been able to find just cause to get rid of Nurse Tyler, he would already have. But since that predecessor was his own mother...until Tyler screwed up royally, he was stuck with her.

She looked different tonight. For one thing, she didn't have on the scrubs that were her normal garb. Well-worn jeans and a thin sweatshirt were it. Made her look smaller, younger, more vulnerable. The dark hair shot through with fiery red was loose around her narrow shoulders, softening her classically beautiful, feline face. The big blue eyes that usually snapped fire at him were quiet and terrified.

That was what got to him the most. The terror. Perci Tyler rarely showed fear—at least not in his presence. She'd rather gnaw off her own arm before letting *him* see she was afraid of something.

Joel looked at him. "Good. You're still here. She...hit her head. She needs checked out. Fast."

"Get her in here. Who exactly *is* she?" He had a few guesses. Though *this* Tyler wasn't one he could recall seeing before. How many more of them were there? That bastard Martin Tyler had dozens of cousins and just as many siblings, didn't he? He'd never asked Perci how closely she was related to Martin; he just knew she was. Same hair, same eyes. Same toxic attitude.

The Tylers of Tyler Township were hard to misidentify, that was for certain. He'd had personal run-ins with a good half dozen of them. Not a pleasant lot, that was for certain.

"She's my older sister, Phoebe." Perci's pretty face turned toward him, her natural wariness where he was concerned right there for him to see.

"How old? Medical history?" He hadn't meant to be so brusque, but something about the Tyler family always brought it out in him. He'd told himself not to hold her family against Perci when he'd first met her. After less than a week, it was *she* who grated on his nerves so badly he bled whenever he was in her presence for too long.

"She's twenty-five, and other than the accident that damaged her hearing when she was five or six, she's not had any major health issues. No allergies, no underlying conditions. She just...hit her head tonight." There was no fire in Perci tonight. Just a look that shot straight through him, a look he'd seen on loved ones' faces before. A look that begged him to make their loved one well again. To *fix* everything again.

Little Perci Tyler was terrified.

So that was what it took to make her quiet. Fear. Nate was man enough to admit he far preferred her *fighting* than *fearing*.

"Let's get her looked at, ok? Joel? You can probably go now. I'll see the Tylers are well taken care of." Joel probably had a dozen other things on his plate at the moment with the entire county on a state of alert for flooding; the floods were slated to hit sometime in the wee hours of the morning, making them doubly treacherous. It was one reason why he was still at the hospital so late. The hospital was a bit too close to the flood plain for his liking. He'd wanted to double-check emergency procedures one more time. Nate looked at his older brother.

He was holding the woman tightly, a look of fear in his own eyes. How was his brother involved with the Tylers? Nate took a closer look at the woman as he indicated for his brother to put her on the exam table. The woman was beautiful and favored her younger sister greatly. Twenty-*five?* That meant *Perci* was several years younger than Nate had originally thought.

The woman opened eyes the same blue as her sister's and looked up at him. The resemblance was strong, but this woman's face was a bit rounder, sweeter than feline like Perci's. "My head hurts...really hurts. Can you put my brains back inside my skull soon, please?" She spoke with the slightly altered tones of one who'd been deaf for a while. Nate checked for hearing devices in both ears; she wore one in her left.

"As soon as we can, Ms. Tyler. Let's get you taken care of, ok? Care to tell me what happened?"

"It's the sheriff's fault. He brought my brother home..." She waved a hand toward Joel, then brought it to the laceration on her temple. "Should have just kept him...much less work that way..."

"And then what?" Was it a domestic-abuse situation? Had someone struck the small woman on the table hard enough to knock her out? The brother, perhaps?

He'd seen it before. He pulled the blanket she was wrapped in back and did a quick visual inspection. She wore a thin cotton robe over most of her body, but he didn't see anything too concerning. Nothing to indicate abuse. And her sister had never shown any of the signs, either. "Someone *hit* you?"

"No. Well, yes. My brother knocked me down. Trying to get to..." She lifted her hand to her head again. She had small hands, Nate noticed, small and pretty. Hands that trembled.

Joel interrupted. "Her brother was drunk, Nate. She got caught in between us, and she came out the loser. Struck her head on a dining room chair leg as she went down. We got her here as quickly as we could, but they live out past Levi's new property."

Their youngest brother, Levi, had just purchased another property near the southern half of the county. It connected to the ranch that had been in their family for more than four generations now, the ranch where the four brothers still lived. Which meant a good thirty-five-minute drive to the hospital—at top speed. "It's possible she has a concussion. More than likely, I'd say. She lose consciousness?"

"Yes. She was out for a moment or two. But she's also been confused since." Joel's worry was hard to miss; nor was the way he hovered over the woman. The woman who apparently blamed him for her injury.

"Then we'll see what's going on."

"Don't worry, Phoebe." Perci leaned over her sister and grabbed the woman's left hand. "He might be a real jerk, but Dr. Masterson knows what he's doing. You'll be fine. I know you will."

"Gee, Tyler, I think that's the nicest thing you've ever said to me." He didn't look at the other woman, just focused on checking the pupils of the smaller one in front of her. Perci Tyler was very petite at around five three—this sister was practically elf-sized.

"Yeah, well. Extenuating circumstances. Don't take it too personally."

The injured sister finally smiled, revealing a smile that could damned well stop traffic. No wonder his brother looked a little shell-shocked.

Nate commiserated. He'd felt the same since he'd met Persephone. Damn her to hell, that woman got to *him*.

6

PHOEBE JUST FOCUSED ON BREATHING—AND trying not to cry. The next two hours were a blur of X-rays and exams. Tests she could definitely not afford. She acquiesced simply because Perci insisted on it and because the sheriff was watching. That man terrified her. Something about the way he looked at her...

"Where's Phoenix?" she asked Perci.

"The sheriff had one of his deputies meet us here. He took Phoenix to jail—on assault charges," her sister said. "Don't you remember?"

Phoebe shook her head gingerly.

"The sheriff tried to catch you. I think he knocked you a little bit—otherwise, you would've hit the edge of the table, Phoebe. Phoenix could've killed you. He's gone too far this time."

Phoebe sighed. "And the sheriff?"

"He just scooped you right up and carried you out to his SUV. And here we are." Her sister helped her off the table at Phoebe's insistence. "You should stay."

"We can't afford it, Perci. You know that. We just...can't. Let's go. You can take care of me at *home*." A thought occurred to her. "How are we going to get there?"

HE WAS GROWING IMPATIENT—WITH THE hospital. With his own brother. Nate was head of the small county hospital. He appreciated Nate handling Phoebe's care personally, but he wished Nate would just hurry it along.

The storms had finally broken free and ranged from Della near the southeastern state line all the way up to where Masterson County met Montana in the northwest part of the state. Joel's cell was already ringing off the hook, demanding his attention. He couldn't stick around the hospital too much longer.

He wanted to. The girl hadn't felt all that substantial when he was carrying her. Not at all. She'd been small, feminine, and far too vulnerable for his liking.

He should have known that idiot brother was too drunk to make rational decisions. He'd practically put her in a position to be hurt himself.

The guilt was what was keeping his ass in the hard orange waiting room chair.

Nate came out of the exam room, a look of consternation on his face.

"What? The Tyler girl?"

"She needs to be watched tonight. But she is refusing to stay."

"Why the hell for?"

"Because she's a *Tyler* and they're stubborn as all hell? Because she can't pay the *bill*, Joel. She was very clear on that. Her sister's helping her dress now."

"Damn it. Doesn't she have insurance?"

"Not on herself, apparently." Nate frowned. He glanced over his shoulder toward the exam room. And then he sighed. "For some, it's cheaper to pay the fine for not having the insurance on their taxes than come up with the monthly premiums. And what the state now offers isn't that great of an alternative. She's young and unmarried, but too old to be on her father's insurance policy. She may not qualify for the income guidelines, *but* the premium could eat up available reserves. I've seen it before. I'd say your girl slipped through the cracks somehow. Most likely deliberately."

"The sister's a nurse, right? What do you know about her?"

"Young, experienced, proud, difficult. Damned difficult. The list goes on. I've dealt with *Persephone* Tyler before. I don't like this—at all. She is gambling with her life here, Joel."

Neither did Joel, but...

"It's her choice. I need to drive them home, but I should have been out in front of these storms hours ago."

"I'll drive them home. I'm on my way out now, anyway."

It was the only solution Joel really had.

He waited until the woman and her slightly taller sister reappeared.

Joel told her exactly what he thought of her stupidity—then he left her for his brother to deal with. He had a county to take care of.

7

Dr. Masterson chose to force his way into their house, and he stayed. Supposedly because of Phoebe's concussion. Phoebe had her own theories—*Perci* had a way of drawing men to her at times.

Perci and the doctor argued from the moment he'd told them he was giving them a ride home to the moment he asked her father if he could stay on their couch to make sure Phoebe didn't need help in the middle of the night.

It was the strangest house call Phoebe had ever heard of. As for Perci, it was very clear that she and the doctor hated each other. And had tangled many times before. Whatever was there between them, it was a big problem.

One that had her head hurting worse than ever before.

She still had to find a way to deal with Phoenix. They couldn't leave him in jail.

Pip, usually ran ragged during the day as it was, somehow also took over the three younger boys' homeschooling. The ranch was too far from the county school sixty miles away. Like a lot of families in Masterson County, they homeschooled. It was only Phoenix in his senior year—though he was nineteen and a year behind because of the wreck that had killed their mother—who attended the county high school.

Because he'd insisted. And their father had given in. Honestly, it was easier to have him gone during the day than at home. There was far too much work to do to deal with Phoenix.

Dr. Masterson refused to let Phoebe out of bed for the entire day. Before he left after breakfast, he gave very clear instructions to Perci and told her to take the day off to stay with her family. That—and the killer headache—nearly drove her insane.

Phoebe had too much work to do to stay in bed all day. With Phoenix gone, that meant there were even more chores to do. The three younger boys did their best to help out, but the ranch was taking everything they had to keep going.

Phoebe lay back against the pillows and fought crying. It seemed like there was always just one more chore to be done. And it never ended.

She closed her eyes, hoping sleep would help her escape for just a little while.

8

JOEL MANAGED FOUR SOLID HOURS OF SLEEP, AT least. It was the best he was going to get, and he knew it. He was at his desk when his brother came in. Nate settled his big body in the chair opposite Joel's and pulled his Stetson from his head. "I stayed at the Tylers' place last night. Kept an eye on that girl for you."

"How is she?" He tried to shove the guilt away, but it wouldn't go anywhere. He should've secured the brother better. Phoebe could have seriously been hurt because of *his* misjudgment. He'd never forget that. Or the way she felt as he'd held her. How pale she had been when he told her how stupid he thought she was for not staying at the hospital. How proud she'd been when she'd asked him if the sheriff's office was going to pay the bill. Told him if not, she wasn't any of his business any longer.

He owed her an apology, and probably more than one. He hadn't exactly handled himself well last night. Not at all. Even thinking of her disconcerted him. It had been blue eyes that he'd dreamed about in the four hours he had slept.

"She'll recover. Most likely. She has one hell of a headache right now."

Nate looked back toward the rear of the station —where the cells were. "Seen a lot of Tylers come to the ER. Trouble; at least ninety percent of them. Didn't realize Persephone Tyler had so many sisters or brothers, though. Don't think I've ever met any of them before. Just her."

"I checked police reports, Nate. Nothing on this Phil Tyler *or* his kids. Except for that one back there. Apparently, he's the worst of the lot. Not even speeding tickets."

"Hmm. Just give them time, I bet. Tylers are *always* trouble of some sort or another. Persephone certainly is." Nate leaned back. "The Tyler boy still back there?"

"Yes." Joel was trying to decide what to do

with the kid. He was too old for juvenile detention, and unless the sister pressed charges for assault, he hadn't done anything serious enough for Joel to keep him. Technically, since Joel had witnessed the assault, the boy should face charges regardless. But since Joel was the only witness, he didn't want to force the issue unless he had to.

Assault charges would stay with the boy for a long, long time.

"You might tell him that not only did he just cost his family a couple grand or more in ER bills, but half an inch toward the left, and it could've killed his sister outright. Something for him to consider. Damned lucky it didn't."

"I grabbed her. Last second. I pulled her closer just before she hit." Joel fought back a sudden rush of nausea at how close it had been.

"You saved her life then. Lucky girl."

Lucky? It never should have happened. He was equally as guilty as Phoenix Tyler.

Joel would never forget that.

9

JOEL COULDN'T DEAL WITH THE TYLER BOY until late the next day. When he finally did, it was to find the boy sullen and morose in his cell.

"Tyler? You doing all right?" It was a small prison located in the northern part of the county building that also contained Joel's office and the entire sheriff's department. It wasn't anything much, just an older facility used to house temporary prisoners and low-risk offenders. A boy in the drunk tank fit right in.

Tyler looked like a pitiful little boy pouting in the corner. All alone in the world. It was hard for Joel to look past that for a moment.

And then he remembered what Nate had told

him. Half an inch difference and the boy would have been facing manslaughter charges for the *death* of his own sister.

How small and vulnerable she had felt when he'd carried her semi-lucid into the ER settled in his mind again. She had clung to him, crying silently.

Phoenix Tyler needed to be taught a lesson. Immediately. Before his stupidity next time *did* get someone else killed.

"I'm fine. When am I getting out of here?"

"Now, see, that depends."

"On what?" No attitude this time. Nothing but a strange apathy. Did the kid truly not care? What was broken in this kid to cause all of this?

"On your *sister*. Personally, I'd charge you with assault myself. That sister of yours could have been seriously hurt. Could have lost the rest of her hearing, did you know that? Not to mention that you could have killed her if I hadn't managed to grab her a bit there as she fell. The doctor says half an inch to the left, and it could have been fatal. And for what? Because of some drunken fight with Tom Rutherford?"

Now that name got a real reaction out of the boy. And not one Joel was expecting. Fear ran through the blue eyes that were so like his sisters'. "Rutherford's a dick!"

"Whatever. I don't *care* what's between you. You had no right to act that way with your family. What if your sister was seriously hurt? Wait a minute—she *was*. A concussion is no laughing matter. She's stuck in bed right now. She *should* be in the hospital, but for some reason, refused to stay. Because *she* doesn't have health insurance and is terrified of another bill. You do; I checked. So if you were the one with a massive headache right now, you'd be getting all the right medical attention. But she's not; did you know that? If something happens, she's forty minutes from *help*. Except for your sister, who had to take the day off of work to take care of her." Joel repeated everything Nate had told him with force, wanting to make his point very clear to the boy. "Now, let me ask you something, Mr. Tyler. If your sisters were *already* struggling to find money to feed your younger brothers, how can they afford for one to take off from the only paying job they have?"

"Screw you."

It wasn't a surprise, the teen's words. He'd been hoping differently, of course. But there was something broken in Phoenix Tyler right now. Anyone could see that.

Joel just didn't know if he could fix it. Or if he should even bother trying.

Until Tyler turned to look at him out of those blue eyes that were just like his sister's.

That woman...

Something about her had stayed with him from the moment he'd left her in the ER in his brother's care.

She hadn't deserved what had happened.

The least her brother deserved was an object lesson for what he had done. "As soon as she's recovered enough to get out of her bed, I'll stop by. Talk to her. See what *she* wants to do. In the meantime, can I get you something to read while you're here? We have *Crime and Punishment* or the Bible. Your choice."

"Go to hell."

"Nope. Right now...I'm going to go see your sister."

He made it to the Tyler ranch just as the sun was setting in the distance. He was met on the front porch by none other than Phoebe herself. She had the youngest boy by the hand. Joel took a close look at the kid for the first time. He looked very much like the rest of his siblings, though the hair was a bit blonder than dark red. He just stared at Joel solemnly.

Finally, the boy spoke. "You come to take my Phoebe to jail, too?"

"Parker, that's enough, sweetie. Go back inside and let me talk to the sheriff, ok? Pip and Pan will have dinner finished in a bit. Why don't you help set the table?"

The child obeyed. The older sister stared at Joel from the relative safety of the porch. Finally, he stepped over the faded stepping stones and stopped just in front of her. Where he could almost reach out and touch her. Even with her a few steps above him, she was short. Small.

He'd never found petite women attractive before. He'd always preferred women who were a lot closer to six feet. Easier to hold that way.

But he'd had his arms around her for a while the night before, and he hadn't had a problem with her small size at all. He could lift her right up off her toes and press his lips to hers easily enough.

If he wanted to, that was.

He cleared his throat and pulled his white hat off his head. He'd been raised to be a gentleman, after all. "Miss Tyler, how are you doing today?"

"Well, I'm out of bed. That's an improvement. How's my brother? When do we need to pick him up?" She was just as wary today as she had been the night before. Joel couldn't blame her. The white bandage on her temple was like a neon sign to his failure to protect.

"That's up to you. I still intend to charge him for the underage drinking and assaulting a police officer. It's up to you if you press charges against him for what happened to *you*."

"Please, don't." She came off the steps and held up her hands between them. *Damn it,* Joel had to force himself not to touch.

"We can't afford this. We just *can't*. Phoenix... he'll need a lawyer, and with the bill from last night, we just can't do it."

It was the tears that did it. Had him wanting to soften the blow. "Here's the deal. I'm *keeping* the underage drinking charge. He needs to know that *that* is a problem. I'll drop the assault charges. He goes to the free counseling at the clinic for anger management *and* alcohol abuse and keeps his nose clean for the next year. A type of probation, just between my office and your family. One screw up and I'll tack on that charge."

"Thank you. Our family...really appreciates it."

"Look, I don't want to cause trouble for your family. I truly don't. I just want to help." Joel stepped closer, almost without thought. He *should* be turning around and heading as far away from this woman as he could get. Instead, he kept moving away from his Denali and closer to her. Like a moth to the light of the moon, or something as equally stupid as that. Phoebe Tyler drew him right in. It had to be the blue eyes. "How's the head?"

She grimaced, one hand brushing the bandage lightly. "Splitting."

"Why are you up so soon? Shouldn't you be resting?" He had to admit she looked a little too pale for his liking. Where did this concern keep coming from?

"Sheriff, if I stay in bed all day resting because of a headache, then the work isn't getting done. The kids needed to eat, do their school, do their chores, the goats needed to be tended, and Perci had to help Pip with a foaling. Dad's up at the back pasture with Pandora and Patton. We just...

have too much to do for me to lay around in bed. With Phoenix gone, there's even more work. Even with Perci taking the day off."

Joel knew as well as she did what she was saying. There was never truly an end to ranch work. There was always going to be just one more chore that could be getting done.

He put his cowboy hat back on his head before he did something stupid, like offer to help her herd goats or something. "Just take it easy, honey. You won't do *anyone* any good if you hurt yourself more because you should have rested. I'm going to head out. I'll be letting your brother out in the morning. I'll see to it he gets a ride home."

"*No.*"

Joel turned toward the man behind him that he hadn't heard approaching. Phil Tyler stood there, an older border collie next to him.

"Mr. Tyler, I stopped by to let your daughter know about your son. He's facing an underage drinking charge. Probation for everything else."

"I heard. And I heard why you're dropping the assault charges. I don't want him here. Not long term. He can gather his things, then I want him *gone*. I stand by what I said. I won't have him here —not until I can trust him to not hurt his brothers or sisters." There was grief in the man's face that Joel couldn't ignore. He felt for Tyler; he had to admit that.

"Daddy, where will he go? We can't just kick him out like a stray dog who got too close to the chickens. He's...family."

The older man stared at his daughter for the longest time. Joel watched as those eyes of hers worked magic on the older man. Just like they had *him* a few moments ago. They really were hard to resist, weren't they?

There was serious power in those eyes.

Finally, the old man relented. "He can stay up at the cabin." He turned to Joel. "We have a small line shack at the back of the ranch. Up the side of the mountain. Tell my son...he can get his things and the cabin's his. He'll tend the pastures and the head we have up that way. In exchange, he'll get free room and board for the next six months. He keeps up his schooling, doesn't cause any trouble, we'll talk then of extending it. And he is *never* to do anything to endanger his sisters—or brothers —again."

It was the best Phoenix Tyler was going to get. Joel just wished he wasn't the one going to deliver the news.

"I'll let him know in the morning."

"Thank you, Sheriff. Phoebe Kate, get yourself inside. I want you to go to bed early. You need the rest. Sheriff, we're about to settle down to dinner. You're welcome to join us. It's not fancy, but we have enough to share."

Joel didn't see how he had any choice. Turning the offer down would be a blow that Phil Tyler didn't deserve. There was such pride in the man's face, such wariness on the daughter's. Such fear. He accepted the offer.

10

PHOEBE DIDN'T WANT HIM AT HER DINNER table. But that was exactly where he was. He took the chair to her left, where Phoenix usually sat. Pip was on *his* left, thankfully. Pip was quiet and accepting enough of anything and anyone that having the very man who'd arrested their brother next to her wouldn't rock Pip's boat.

Phoebe definitely couldn't say the same. She could even *smell* the scent of him right there next to her. She'd never smelled her brother when he sat next to her. At least, not in a good way. Not like this. And whenever he moved, the brush of his arm against hers sent shock waves from her skin to her brain.

Turned her already aching brain into total mush.

She disguised her response by focusing on her brothers. Parker and Patton were terrified of the sheriff in their midst. Their father and brother—and even Perci and Phoebe—hadn't had many positives to say about the man who'd occupied that position before *this* sheriff had been elected in his place. He'd harassed her family off and on for years before losing in a landslide election to this man.

Sheriff Clive Gunderson had made no secret of the fact that he considered all Tylers worthless troublemakers.

Yes, that was true for a lot of her cousins—her father was one of twelve children, mostly boys; she had *a lot* of cousins roaming the county—but it wasn't true of *all* of them. It definitely wasn't true for *her* branch of the Tyler family tree. Sheriff Gunderson hadn't ever been able to understand that.

Unfortunately, that experience had left its mark on her entire family.

No one wanted the sheriff right there in their home. No one. Thankfully, Perci was the only one to say anything even remotely antagonistic.

The sheriff just ignored her. Perci had long had an issue with her boss at the hospital. She'd told the entire family about him, repeatedly. None of them had realized he was the sheriff's brother, though. Until yesterday. After everything that had happened with Phoenix, Perci was doubly hostile.

If Phoebe's head wasn't hurting so badly, she probably would be, too.

As it was, they made it through dinner. The sheriff was polite, appreciative, and well-mannered. He smiled at the children several times, and he listened to them when they did speak.

He engaged Pandora in a light conversation about working online. He was kind to Pip and seemed to understand that the younger twin was extremely shy. He did nothing to overwhelm. He even seemed to find some of Perci's pointed barbs humorous.

It was the way he *looked* at Phoebe that had *her* on edge.

She was ready for the sheriff of Masterson County to just get gone.

11

Joel drove Phoenix Tyler back to the Tyler ranch the next morning. He was met at the front porch by Phoebe and her youngest sister. She had lighter red hair than Phoebe, was about four inches taller and twenty-five pounds heavier. She had the same sweet, heart-shaped face and slightly darker blue eyes.

If *she* was old enough to drink, he'd eat his white hat. The two women watched their brother warily like they expected him to erupt right there in the midst of him.

Instead, Phoenix just looked at his eldest sister and the bandage still on her forehead. "I'm sorry. It was stupid what I did. Didn't mean to hurt you."

Phoebe came down the steps quickly. She hugged her brother. "I know. I'm sorry about all this, too."

The boy's chin rose. "I'm not. Time I left this place behind. I can take care of myself."

Joel bit back a snort. Sure the kid could. While still living on Daddy's back forty. With those four pretty sisters of his probably bringing him Crock-Pots full of food each week.

Sure the kid could.

Hell, by the time *his* youngest brother Levi had been nineteen ten years ago, Joel was already working as a deputy, Nate was through with med school, Matt was through with veterinary school, and *Levi* was set to take over the day-to-day operation of the Masterson spread. After they were done with the day at their full-time jobs, Matt, Joel, and Nate had been out there right next to Levi helping run the place.

Now Levi had expanded that spread twice in the last five years.

Nothing at all like this kid, was it?

He waited while the kid and the youngest sister packed the boy's belongings. Phoebe handed the kid keys. "Dad said...you'll need the truck. To get to school and back. You have to keep up your grades, or it's no deal."

"I can handle myself just fine, Phoebe."

"I know. But...you're my brother. I guess I never imagined one of us would eventually move out. Silly, huh? Figured we'd all stay here forever. At least until someone got married, anyway."

"Have to date to get married first," the youngest sister said.

"Hush, Pan."

The taller girl just waved nonchalantly. There was a bite in her tone when she spoke to her brother. "See you around, Phoenix. Don't forget to write."

"Yeah, you, too. Keep an eye on this place, will you?"

"Always do." Pan patted her brother on the shoulder then took off around the back of the house. Her action told Joel one thing—*she* wasn't the least upset to see her brother go.

Within two minutes the boy climbed into the truck that was older than he was, and was gone.

Leaving Joel right there next to Phoebe.

Alone.

When she sighed and turned toward him, Joel looked down into those soul-stealing blue eyes.

Those suspiciously wet blue eyes. "Hey, it's not like he's moving to Michigan or something. He's what? A few miles north of here?"

"You have a large family, Sheriff?"

"Hmmm. I have my mother—who is off somewhere in an RV taking travel photos while on sabbatical from the hospital—and I have my three younger brothers. Several cousins."

"Like we Tylers."

"Honey, I don't think there's a bigger family in the county than you Tylers."

"Yes, there are a lot of us. But in *this* branch, we've had each other's backs for the past two years. *Especially* Phoenix's. To have him leave, even though it makes things easier, hurts. What if your brothers left?"

"It would hurt. We share the family homestead—when we're not all off working. We don't tend to work traditional hours, I'm afraid. Only Levi, the youngest of us, works the ranch full time."

"Then you do understand. I've taken care of the kids in this house since *before* my mother died. To see one of them go like this...I understand why my father is doing this." She touched her head again almost unconsciously. "I really do. It's just..."

"He's your brother, and you love him." Joel brushed a hand over her back softly. She didn't pull away. "But he's not really that far away. And I'm sure you'll be checking on him a dozen times a day for a while, right? So why did you take care of the kids back then? When did your mother pass away?"

"Two years ago. In a car...accident. But after she had Parker, she had a rough time recovering. I was able to come home from college and help out. Patton was only two, and Pete six."

It sank in then. They were more her children than her siblings, weren't they? No wonder she seemed so much the heart of her family. She did the cooking and the cleaning and raised the children, while the rest of their family did what they could to bring in the money for them all to survive. Each and every Tyler was so integral to the others that it was no wonder seeing one on such a destructive path as Phoenix hurt her.

Joel shocked the hell out of himself when he wrapped his arms around her and hugged her. "It'll be ok, honey. All of us have to learn to be adults sometime. Now is as good a time as any for your brother. And if it'll help, I'll keep an eye on him myself when I can. I promise."

HE SMELLED LIKE WOODS AND SUN AND MAN.
That overrode all sense of shock she felt. It had
been a *long* time since Phoebe had been close
enough to an attractive man to notice how good he
smelled. How strong his arms were. To hear the
steady beat of his heart beneath her cheeks. She
was pressed full-length against the sheriff. How
had that even happened? Phoebe didn't know, but
she wasn't sure she liked it.

Or sure that she *didn't* like it, for that matter.

Sometimes it was nice to be held by someone
who wasn't seven years old and covered with grape
jelly.

She pulled back a little and looked up at him.
"Sheriff...I..."

"It'll all be ok, honey. I promise..." He lowered
his head a little. Just enough to brush his lips over
hers slightly.

The wooden screen door slammed open behind her, and someone called her name. It was
enough to have her springing from his arms and
heading back toward the house.

Where her family waited.

12

PARKER WAS THE ONE WHO FOUND THE BLOOD. It scared the little boy so much that it took Phoebe more than an hour to calm him down—and the rest of her family. Who would do such a thing? Why? And what was it? It wasn't one of her goats. She and Pan had gone outside with their father's rifles and counted. No, all forty of her little drove were still safe.

It had to have been a cat or a squirrel. Or something like that.

That wasn't the worst part.

It was the chilling message, written in the animal's blood, that told them so much. That had her ordering Pan to call the sheriff's office and request

Joel Masterson personally. It still took the sheriff two hours to get to them. By the time he finally arrived, she was sick, angry at the monster who'd done it so near her little brothers, and terrified.

She went to the front door to meet the sheriff. Phoebe shaded her eyes with one hand and watched as the long, tall sheriff climbed out of the SUV. Joel—hard to think of a man as the *sheriff* when he'd kissed her in her front yard—was well over six-foot-something tall, broad-shouldered, lean, and—*well*—*beautiful* with his dark hair and dark-green eyes.

"What's happened? Why'd you call my office? Is it Phoenix?"

She shook her head, unsure what to say next. "You'll need to come with me. This way."

She didn't want him there, didn't want *him* specifically seeing this; too much family history with the sheriff's office of this county made her leery of asking for help from Masterson County. *This* put him in an official capacity. No matter if he had kissed her just eight days ago.

She was a Tyler, and in this part of the country, that meant something, and not always in a good way. Had someone mistaken *their* ranch for one of their cousins' or uncles'? It was possible.

She knew the reputation her uncles and cousins and even her grandfather had, but not *her* family. Her family kept to themselves. They didn't deserve to be treated like this.

It was hard to forget that if she had called Sheriff Gunderson about this, she would have been kept waiting possibly indefinitely. She didn't think *this* sheriff was like that, though. It was still hard to trust him. If she just knew what it was the man wanted from her...knew why he'd kissed her that way...*then* she could deal with that and separate the *sheriff* from the *man.* Right?

"It is about blood. Threats."

"What the hell are you talking about?" He strolled up to her, and she could see the visible impatience in his movements. It took everything she had not to back away from the large animal stalking toward her. "Honey, you're not very clear. And I got *a lot* going on back in town right now."

"I'm sorry. I...Come with me, you'll see for yourself. My youngest brother found it. It took you two hours to get here." Two hours when she had forced herself not to freak out because she and Pan were alone in the house with two of their brothers and that *mess* was out on her porch.

"I was clear across the county on a drug bust. No one told me your call was urgent."

"Good thing I know how to shoot a rifle. Because if anything ever happened, God knows we're too far away to count on your office for help." She shivered as that sank in yet again. She and Pan and the boys had been alone while that monster was out there, so close...

Phoebe turned her back on him and walked around the house to the back where it was. He needed to do whatever it was he was supposed to do, and then get gone. She'd need to decide how to tell her father so it wouldn't upset him. And then she, the twins, and Pan would have to decide what to do about this. The way they had handled everything life had thrown at them since the moment they'd lost their mother. "This way."

13

THE WOMAN JUST GOT BETTER EVERY TIME HE looked at her. Joel didn't see that changing anytime soon. The clothes were cheap and faded from lots of washing, but they didn't hide the truth. She had her dark-red hair pulled up in an intricate French braid. *This* Tyler of Tyler Township, though small and as fiery as all those cousins of hers, was damned beautiful.

And frightened. He'd seen her frightened before. It was not an expression he was going to forget anytime soon.

Joel took a look around the ranch in the daylight. They'd started painting it sometime in the last week. They were making improvements, though it was going to take them time. It was obvious they didn't have two dimes to rub together for much of anything else, but they were hardworking and determined.

There was strain around her eyes, a strain that shouldn't be there for one so young. The curtain moved, and he looked up to see two young boys staring out the window at him. "No school?"

"Homeschool. We've finished for the day. I'd just sent Parker outside to play after his math when he came running back in. He slipped in the blood. He's not quite *eight*."

Joel saw what she meant. The garish red across the fresh white paint was hard to miss. *Time to pay up. You little sluts are going down.*

Written in blood. Of that, he had no doubt. Part of the animal's entrails was sitting there on the welcome mat. Joel didn't know whether to be sick or pissed.

Pissed won. Joel swore under his breath.

"Where is your father?" Joel was surprised the older man wasn't nearby, a rifle at the ready to defend his family if needed.

"He and my sisters are in the back pasture bringing down some horses. We have potential buyers coming out this afternoon. Dad doesn't know about *this*. Neither do Pip or Perci. I'd like to have it taken care of as soon as possible."

"Who are the buyers?"

"I'm not sure, Pip handles everything to do with the horses. The goats are mine. My father handles everything else with the ranch. We're doing the best we can, but it's slow going. My sister put an ad up somewhere, and a man called yesterday wanting to see the cutting horses she's trained."

"You vet this guy? Sure he's legit?"

"I'm sure Pip did. We're not stupid, Sheriff. Even if we are Tylers."

"I never said anything about you being Tylers." Tylers had an illustrious history going back at least two hundred years. Joel understood that. But damn it, it was just a last name. Not a predisposition to strife. Whenever there was a Tyler involved, the rumor had, there was bound to be trouble, though.

The woman in front of him was certainly trouble. To *him*, anyway. He hadn't been able to forget her in the week since he'd said to hell with everything and kissed those pretty lips of hers.

"Where's Phoenix at today?"

"He's been cooperating. He goes to school. He

tends to that corner of the property. And that's it. My father will not allow him back in the house for anything. He didn't have anything to do with this if that's what you're thinking. Just forget that. Phoenix would never harm an animal. Besides, he's really squeamish. Even the sight of a paper cut bleeding is enough to make him gag. Phoenix wouldn't do this." She crossed her arms over her chest, which wasn't very big but still drew his eyes, and glared up at him. She looked like an enraged fairy. It was the fear in her blue eyes that kept eating at him. He couldn't stand to see a woman afraid.

"Do you have any idea who would?"

She shook her head. "No. To be honest, we stick to ourselves. We know what it means to be a Tyler in this county. Former Sheriff Gunderson made that all very clear to us years ago. My father made a vow when he was not much older than Patton, who is eleven, that he would not end up like his brothers. He stuck to that. He's raised us not to be like them, either. We work hard, we take care of each other, and we try not to make trouble. That's it. This..." She waved a hand toward the porch.

He watched the shiver go right through her, and before he realized he was even moving, Joel put his hand on her shoulder and squeezed. Just to comfort. To let her know that she wasn't alone. She felt so small beneath his touch. How much of this family did she carry on her shoulders? Who did she really have?

Yes, there were a lot of Tylers. Her father? He just seemed like a man who was overwhelmed by everything, working hard to make the ranch profitable. But everyone knew that ranching around these parts was not a magic bullet or lottery ticket. Very few succeeded more than just eking by. Her sisters? They were even younger. How much help could they really be? Wouldn't they all naturally look to her as the eldest for advice, for help?

They were just learning their own way in the world, too.

Four boys? Seems like she was raising three of them herself. "Tell me about this place, honey. Seems like you have a lot of irons in the fire."

"Hopefully, they'll start paying out *soon*. I have forty Angoras. We shear them ourselves and sell the mohair for custom yarn making. Or I use the yarn myself. I weave and sell my creations online. Pan manages my site and all sales. Pip is busting her rear to start her own breeding program for cutting horses, American quarter horses. She trains them, too. We're going to try to sell off two of them today to pay my hospital bill. And beef up our savings account. Perci helps, her paycheck. It's needed. And then when she's not at the hospital, she's out helping Pip. Or helping my father with the cattle. I handle the goats, the boys, and the house. See, we've not done a damn thing to hurt anyone. We've done nothing that would explain *this*."

"No, I never thought you would've. So who could be holding a grudge against your family?" Joel brushed his hand down her arm until he could grasp her fingers in his. He turned her away from the bloody sight on the porch. "Show me the rest of your operation."

"Give me a minute." She stepped inside the house through a side door. He heard her yell at the boys to finish the chores, and then she returned. "This way. I need to be back before Pip's buyers arrive. Pip and Perci and my father will need help. And I want to be here when my father learns of this. His heart's not the greatest."

"I'm going to have to interview your sisters. That message is pretty distinct. *Sluts* generally implies female. And you are all four definitely *little*. Four of you have any boyfriends, ex or otherwise, who may be angry over something? Rivals for the same men, possibly?"

"We don't date. None of us."

Joel didn't fully believe that. They were beautiful women in a county where women, in general, were outnumbered two-to-one. And no man had been interested in the four Tyler sisters? He found that a little hard to understand.

"Why is that? Look, somebody somewhere has a grudge against your family. Unless this is a prank. That's a pretty sick prank. So unless one of your sisters or *you* have pissed off some guy, maybe spurned one unknowingly? Or some guy wants to be more than what he currently is to one of you? I don't have any answers. Yet. I will get them for you, honey."

Big blue eyes looked up at him. For some reason, he didn't think she had much faith in him. And that struck a chord in him somehow.

Before he could say anything, a black truck pulled in behind his Denali. One he recognized. She looked at it, too. "That has to be our buyers."

"Possibly. I do know that it's *my* brother Matt. That's his truck. And probably my brother Levi—" The doors opened, and three tall men climbed out. "Well, looks like it's *all* of us. Including Nate."

"I see. I...what are you going to do about this? Anything? Or should we just carry our rifles with us everywhere we go? And how soon can I get this cleaned up? My family doesn't need to see this anymore."

Quiet as she seemed to be, Phoebe Tyler didn't beat around the bush with things. She certainly didn't pull her punches, and Joel appreciated that. "There really isn't much we can do right now, honey. Nobody saw anything. Yes, it's a threat. But at this point, I don't have anything else to go on. I'll talk to your sisters."

He did take a few quick photos first. Just in case. He considered getting a forensic tech out there to dust for prints, but at this point, it would take weeks or months for everything to get processed at the state lab. As gruesome as it was, this wasn't enough to warrant the expense to the county.

He didn't have to like it, but it was just the way it was.

"I'll see what I can do. That's all I can say."

"It's better than nothing." She told him, bluntly. "If you'll excuse me, I have work. I need to check my goats. And be ready when my sisters get down with the horses. I need to make sure the boys are doing their chores. Thank you for coming out here today. I'll let you know...if anything else *we* can't handle ourselves happens."

"I'm going to go talk to my brothers. Stick around to talk to your sisters. Your father."

"Can I clean up the blood? It needs to be gone, and soon."

"Let me take some more photos first. Listen, I can get someone out here to take prints. But to be honest, it's a long shot. And I doubt it would yield any results, at least not quick enough to do much good here. Chances of getting a good print, and then matching that print to someone already in the system, next to nothing. I can already tell you that. But I'm willing to have someone do it. I'm not trying to brush this off, and I'm going to look into it myself. I'm going to keep you safe, honey. You and your family. I promise you that."

"I'll take your word for it. Right now I just need it *gone*."

Her voice broke, and Joel felt like a complete ass that he couldn't promise her magic bullets and everything all pretty and neat again.

"I got kids inside. They don't need to see this. There's too much work to do right now, anyway.

Thanks again for coming out all this way, Sheriff. Have a good day."

She left him there. Like he'd disappointed her.

Hell, of course he had.

He was the sheriff. She was supposed to be able to depend on him to keep her *safe*. He would try to find the person responsible; he made her a silent promise of that. In the meantime, he'd ramp up his patrols in this area. Just to be on the safe side. He stalked over to his brothers. "What are you three doing here?"

"Same could be asked of you. Tylers causing trouble again?" Nate asked. Joel got it—he did. Martin Tyler and Nate had despised each other for years. Unfortunately, it made Nate untrusting of *every* Tyler in the county.

Joel half felt sorry for the sister who worked with his brother. No doubt Nate was a little harder on her than he should've been.

"Not causing it, *in* it. Someone is harassing them. I'm going to find out who, and why." Joel waved a hand to the porch. His brothers all cursed, seeing what was written there. Seeing the two small women busy with a mop and a bucket and a trashcan. When they saw the young boys coming around the edge of the house to where their sisters were, Phoebe waved the children away sharply, turning her body to block the grisly sight from those kids.

"Who are *they*?" Matt asked.

"Youngest brothers. The way I take it, the four sisters and the father are doing everything they can to keep this place going. And it's not happening yet. You guys here to look at the horses? Well, if you buy today, it's going toward the medical bill from the last time I was out here."

"It's that tight?" Nate asked.

"Apparently."

"Any idea who did that?" Matt asked, pointing at the house. "We're here because we saw the ad in the paper for the quarter horses for sale. Terrence Jonson vouches for this Pip Tyler. I've never met the guy, but—"

"*Girl.* Pip is short for *Philippa*. She's one of the twins. They're identical; the other one is a nurse. She and Nate know each other."

"Not my choice," Nate said, quietly. "*Mother* hired her. But she does her job. And nurses are in such shortage around here I don't have any other choice but to keep her on. Even if she is a Tyler. Hell, she's the first to volunteer for overtime."

"Look, Nate, I know you have a problem with

Tylers, but *this* branch of the family is different. They keep their heads down and do their jobs. They take care of each other. They're not like Martin Tyler and the rest of his crew. Just keep that in mind." Joel looked toward the east at the sound of horses. Two beautiful geldings came into sight, led by two equally beautiful young women.

Joel looked back at his brothers, not missing the sudden appreciation in their eyes. Phil Tyler's daughters were a sight to behold; that was for certain. All four of them.

He frowned. Was that what it was?

Had their refusal to date caught one of them some of the *wrong* kind of attention? "Don't judge them all just by their last name. This family's barely hanging on. That overtime she volunteers for might very well be all the *grocery* money they get each week; understand what I'm saying? Don't make it worse for them."

A minute later the two geldings neared the back fence. And then the twins were there. All of the Tyler sisters greatly resembled each other. The twins were taller and a little heavier than Phoebe. By a few inches and fifteen pounds or so. Their hair was a little shorter than Phoebe's.

One twin dismounted and approached the men. "Which one of you is Matt?"

"Which one are you?" Joel asked. He hadn't quite figured out yet how to tell them apart. He *thought* this was the quieter one, though.

It was Nate who answered. "*Not* Perci. She has a small scar over her left eyebrow."

The twin eyed Nate warily. "Yes. Hello, Dr. Masterson. Perci has a scar. The only noticeable outward difference between us. How can I help you gentlemen today? Sheriff, why are you here?"

"*We* are here to see the horses. Well, Nate, Levi, and I are. Joel's here for something else." Matt said, holding out his hand to the young woman. She shook his hand solemnly. Pip, the quiet, shy one who'd sat next to Joel at dinner. He hadn't quite figured her secrets out yet, either.

The same fear and distrust were in her blue eyes that had been in her older sister's earlier. Maybe more. Joel looked over at her twin. The one he now knew was Perci was eyeing the four of them like they were snakes in the midst of a family of tiny mice. Especially Nate. So wary, so untrusting, these girls. He didn't quite understand it.

"Where're Phoebe and Pan?" Perci asked. "And the boys?"

"We're here, Perci. Where's Dad?" the youngest sister asked from behind Joel. He turned to look at her quickly. His gaze went past the two women toward the porch. They'd worked quickly.

"Sky Dancer wasn't cooperating. Pete stayed behind to walk her back. Dad's coming along with some cattle. I think Sky's missing you today," the other twin said. "What's the sheriff doing here? Is Phoenix all right?"

"Everything's fine," Phoebe said, firmly. "We'll talk later, the *four* of us. Something's happened. We'll deal with it *later*."

Something significant passed between the sisters. Joel wondered just how often they dealt with things just the four of them. Something about this family struck a chord in him. Made him wonder.

Made him want to help. To protect. And not just Phoebe.

Her sisters were too young to be facing the wolves of life out there. Not to mention those kids staring at them all from the porch.

He stuck around and watched as the sisters put the two young horses through their paces, demonstrating some serious skill and training. The animals were well worth the asking price. He knew Matt, who ran his own small cattle and horse operation off the property he'd inherited from one of their great-grandfathers, was seriously impressed. When the demonstration was done, the twin girls dismounted and walked over to the fence where Joel and his brothers, as well as their two sisters, waited.

"You sure you want to see these horses go?" Levi asked. Joel knew what he meant. These horses were younger than what he'd expected. If they waited a year or so to sell them, they could probably command a much higher price.

There was a sadness on Pip's pretty face. "Yes. It *needs* to be done."

Joel understood what she wasn't saying. Money was just that tight, and all of them knew it. Phoebe, behind him, let out a curse so low he doubted anyone else heard. He looked over his shoulder at her, saw the guilt and pain on her face.

She was blaming herself, and he knew it. But they were resolute, and he watched as Matt agreed. As Matt and quiet little Pip shook on the deal. She'd handle the paperwork, she said. And then it was done.

Nate hadn't said much, but his eyes had followed the other twin as she rode the horse. As she dismounted the horse. As she stood there, letting her sister talk.

In fact, Joel didn't think Nate had looked away *from* her since the moment she'd rode in. Interesting. Matt set up a time to come back to pick up the horses. And then Joel's brothers took off after shooting significant looks at Joel.

They weren't the only ones who looked at him. Phoebe stared at him for a long moment. "Don't you have other places to be now, Sheriff?"

One of the twins said her name. Chastising. But she didn't look away from him. He had to admit he liked that she didn't back down. That she quietly challenged him when she could.

Oh, he knew that he scared her. It was in the way she pulled away from him whenever he got too close. It was in the way he remembered her looking at him the night he'd arrested her brother. But there was something else there, something he had yet to put his finger on.

He suspected that she was just as attracted to him as he was her. She wasn't about to let him make the move that he wanted to, nor was she about to make a move of her own. As far as she was concerned, the sheriff of Masterson County was her enemy, and she wanted nothing to do with

do for a prank. Even one with a serious grudge. But to be honest, he didn't have any other leads.

He'd made a point the day after the message to track down each sister individually and ask about possible culprits. All had confirmed what Phoebe had told them. They didn't date, though several had been asked out recently. They just focused on their family as much as possible. None had any arguments with anyone—except Perci with his brother Nate. But he ruled Nate out pretty quickly. Matt and Levi were a pretty tight alibi, and his brother had been with them from the early morning hours.

The three youngest Tyler brothers weren't even old enough to drive. They didn't do much with the people in Masterson—the Tylers preferred to cross county lines and socialize there, rather than in Masterson. So that left only one potential lead.

The teenager with a grudge.

It seems like his best bet would be to start interviewing, and the first one he wanted to speak with was none other than Phoenix Tyler himself.

The high school beckoned. Phoenix Tyler was supposed to be there right now.

15

PHOENIX TYLER HADN'T BEEN TO SCHOOL IN two days. That concerned him. Made him wonder. Had the kid gone off the deep end, wanted to frighten his family for banishing him? Had he done it, then regretted it, so was now hiding?

A bit strange, considering it had been close to a week since it had happened.

He had to juggle looking into the threat with the biggest drug bust in Masterson County history, but he did his best. No one had seen anyone who didn't belong near the Tyler ranch. No one in town had anything bad to say about Phil Tyler and his pretty daughters. In fact, most people didn't even know the man had more than two children—

Phoenix and Perci. The rest kept to themselves so much that half their neighbors didn't even realize they existed.

Why did he find that so odd? He doubted they'd been kept isolated at that ranch. Far from it; Perci had attended college somewhere. As had Phoebe for a while. The youngest sister Pandora had mentioned having her own associate's degree from the small community college in the county directly south of the Tylers' ranch. That was probably it. They lived in Masterson County but didn't act a part of it.

He'd made a point of stopping out there every day, just to do a security check—and always on his own way home. It was being a good sheriff; that's what he told himself.

He knew the truth. He needed to check on her for himself. Whether she welcomed his attention or not.

The problem was *finding* her, at times. The woman worked like a mule, and her sisters were just as bad. Perci left every afternoon at two to clock in at the hospital by three. She'd work her twelve hours—then drive home *alone* at three a.m. Joel wasn't too fond of that idea at all. It made at least one Tyler pretty damned vulnerable. Before

Perci left each day, she'd do twice a single person's chores around the ranch. Pan was also out quite a bit, building her own cleaning service. He understood she also worked online for people needing a secretary. Not to mention her own share of the ranch chores. Pip was most often outside, right alongside her father. Dawn to dusk.

Not a one of those women slouched off in any way. Joel found, in the hour or so Phoebe permitted him to hang around the ranch, that he liked each and every one of them. They didn't seem to stop for anything.

They were going to have to eventually. Before they wore themselves clear down to the bone.

He stopped off five days after the message first appeared. He'd found nothing in all of that time. Other than the fact that Phoenix Tyler wasn't exactly where he was supposed to be.

And his name had just come up as a person of strong interest in Joel's drug-bust case.

Time to find out why.

16

SHE HEARD AN SUV PULL UP, AND PHOEBE paused in her weaving to look out the window of the little shed that was all *hers*. For some reason, it didn't surprise her to see the familiar SUV pulling in. Other than Perci and Pan's cars, and their father's old truck, no other vehicles had been down their drive since the day the sheriff's brothers had purchased Pip's horses. Phoebe liked it that way.

Although she half expected his brothers to show up today, too. Matt Masterson was set to pick up the two horses he'd purchased from Pip in less than an hour.

She walked outside to meet the sheriff, after making sure the boys were still sitting at the table working on their math assignments as she had ordered them. They were good boys. They worked hard, obeyed, and didn't ruffle any feathers. They cared about each other.

She wasn't their mother, but she was the closest thing to one they had now, and she knew it. She'd never take that responsibility lightly. They'd probably be the closest things to children of her own she'd ever have.

Phoebe couldn't see any man willing to take on a family like hers. Nor did she see abandoning her family by marrying someone. And she didn't exactly go too many places to meet men who weren't her cousins. The last attractive men she had met... well...the eldest was walking toward her past her little yellow flowers at that very moment. "Sheriff, what can I do for you today?"

"I stopped off at the school to have a word with your brother. He wasn't there."

"Why do you need him for?" She stared at him, wishing the hat didn't shade his face from her. Wished she could see his eyes, try to figure out what he wanted now. "He do something?"

He looked at her solemnly. "My *drug* investigation, Phoebe. I really need to speak with him."

"I see. Anything I can help you answer?" She

refused to worry about her brother. Phoenix had made his own bed—it was time he learned to lie in it. Harsh as that may seem, her father was right. They had coddled him too much since the accident. Tried to make him see that it wasn't his fault. Not really.

Perci was very adamant on that, even though the accident report said Phoenix had swerved into the other woman's lane. Perci still insisted that it was the *other* way around and that Phoenix was driving carefully. Tom Rutherford's wife was the one to strike them.

Phoenix wouldn't talk about the wreck at all. But who was she supposed to believe? She'd *always* believe her sister first. If Perci said it was Rutherford's wife, then it was Rutherford's wife, and that was the end of it all for her.

"His name has come up in my drug investigation, Phoebe. I need to speak with him alone. As soon as possible."

"He's not here, Sheriff. He's not. We haven't seen him in days."

"I need to see his room."

Now, she wasn't stupid. He didn't have a warrant. Anything he found in Phoenix's room could be used against him. As much as she wanted her brother to face his own problems, she wasn't about to make it easier on the sheriff. Her brother was still her brother, and he was just a confused kid. "You don't have a warrant, *Sheriff*."

"No, I don't." He stepped up onto the porch. He surprised her when he wrapped those big hands of his around her arms and just stood there, holding her. One of his thumbs caressed the soft skin of her inner elbow, and she shivered. Phoebe looked up at him.

This man confused her on so many levels. She didn't know what she was supposed to do next. "I can't let you in. Not like this."

He nodded. "I understand, honey. But I *will* have to get a warrant. It'll get all over town why. We both know how it works around here. Either you give me permission to go in, or I do that. And people around here will know..."

"I—I..." She looked back toward the house, where four sets of blue eyes were staring at her. Staring at him through the open door. What was she supposed to do? She shifted closer to the big man in front of her. Her fingers splayed over his chest. Phoebe felt his heart beating up against her hand. It wasn't fair that a man like him be built like this.

Joel Masterson had it all going for him—handsome, successful well-off, the man wanted for nothing. And now he was asking her to *willingly* let him violate the safety of her home. How was she supposed to do that? What kind of example was it giving to the boys?

Yet if Phoenix had done something, did she really want the boys to see her covering it up for him? Or did she want them to see her going to bat for one of them? She wished her father was home instead of off somewhere selling some cattle. "You get five minutes in his room. you can look, not touch. And *I'll* be in there with you. But you're not going to find anything; he took all of his possessions up to the line shack. He's not here, Sheriff. He's not."

"Just let me look, and I'll be satisfied. And then I'll drive up there. Have words with him myself. How's that, sweetheart?"

Sweetheart? Honey? Well, *honey* she could understand. A lot of the men around here still called women *honey*, even if it wasn't appreciated. But *sweetheart* seemed far more intimate. More intimate than she wanted to think about. It was then that she realized she was practically in his arms again, for all of her brothers and Pan to see.

Phoebe jumped back. "I'm...Phoenix's room was the last one down the hall. Mine is right next to it. The twins are across the hall. Pan has attic access through their room. Pip is going to be moving into Phoenix's room this weekend when we have time to paint and move her stuff. I don't think she's done any cleaning in there yet. We just haven't had the time."

He followed her down the narrow hall. She was aware of his footsteps behind her, every step they took.

Hell, maybe she did need to start going to town more? It didn't have to be Masterson, either. There were other towns just as close. They even went to church just over the county line. That's what she needed to do. Meet people, meet *men*, so that this one didn't overwhelm her so much every time she saw him.

Of course, she had met his brothers recently. None of them had made her feel quite like this. No, so it must just be the sheriff that did it. That disconcerted her so much. She opened the door to what had been Phoenix's room and waved him in. "This is it. It's not much. And you're not going to find anything."

He stepped into the room, and she knew what

he thought. Phoenix's narrow twin bed, with the outdated headboard and footboard that had most likely come from a yard sale back when she was too young to remember, dominated. The walls were dark blue. Pip had planned to paint them a lighter blue paint that they had gotten at the discount store a few days earlier. It hadn't happened yet. There was only one other piece of furniture in the room, a battered old dresser. It still had the peeled backs of stickers stuck to it from where Phoenix had placed Power Ranger decals years earlier. It wasn't much. Probably nothing at all like what the sheriff was used to.

Then again, the Tyler ranch wasn't much to look at, though they were working hard to make it that way again. It was home. And to Phoebe, it always would be.

17

HE WONDERED IF SHE REALIZED THAT SHE WAS close enough for him to practically breathe her in. It was the time he admitted it—Joel was *more* than just fiercely attracted to the fiery woman next to him. She drew him more than any woman he'd ever met.

He was even starting to dream about her at night. The things his subconscious wanted to do to her...

Well, his mother had raised him to be a gentleman, so he shoved *those* thoughts away for a moment. He jammed his hands into his pockets, not to keep himself from touching anything in the room, but to keep himself from touching her. The idea that her room was just right there nearby...

"Can I open the drawers?"

"Do you honestly think if my brother was doing something, he'd leave it in the drawers for one of us to find? Phoenix is highly intelligent. Something you need to keep in mind, Sheriff."

Damn it, he didn't want her to just see him as the sheriff. Not any longer. "It's *Joel*, Phoebe. Not just *Sheriff*. My name is Joel, and I am a man. Use it."

"Why? You tell everyone you're searching their house to call you by your first name? Or am I just the lucky one?"

It was the snark in her tone that did it. Did she even *hear* it? She had to, right? He checked quickly, to see if any of her brothers had followed them. None had. Joel wrapped his hands around her waist and lifted. And then she was eye-to-eye with him. He had a foot and four inches on this woman. At least one hundred and fifty pounds.

He had a strange feeling she could knock him to the floor with very little effort. All she had to do was smile again, smile right at him. He was quickly losing all control, and it all centered on her. "*Why?*

Because I want to hear you say it. I want to know that you're looking at me and not just seeing the damned sheriff. You need to understand something, Phoebe Kate; even as the *sheriff*, I have *nothing* against your family. Nothing against *you*. Yes, we met under a pretty crappy circumstance. I won't deny that. Yes, your brother's made things difficult for us. But that doesn't stop the fact that when I'm near you, I want your eyes on me. I want you seeing *me*, the man. Not the stupid badge. Can you do that?"

"Why?" She didn't want to sound like a broken record, but she had no idea what the man wanted from her. What did he expect? Almost every time she had seen him had been because of something her brother had done, or something that was done *to* her family.

None of what he wanted made sense. If she could even figure out what he wanted in the first place. She had to admit, her experience with men was limited. She wasn't a virgin, but she wasn't exactly *experienced*, either. A man like Joel Masterson—he overwhelmed and confused her just by *breathing*. "Why is it so important to you?"

"Because of *this*." He put her back on her feet. Then he reached out with one hand and quietly closed the bedroom door. His other hand slipped behind her, going around her waist. He pulled her up against him. Her hands went across his chest. Once again, she felt the steady thump of his heart against her fingers. Felt the muscles beneath his denim shirt, felt the strength in him as he held her.

Phoebe didn't like feeling this vulnerable.

Too many times in her life she had felt exactly like that. First as a small child who could barely hear. Then as a woman faced with the prospect of raising five siblings after the death of her mother. And as a *Tyler*. She'd been looked down on by some, including the former sheriff, for her entire life simply because of her last name. Just another reason she preferred her goats to town.

Add in the fact that most adults were larger than she was, and it was a powder keg of *vulnerability*. One that she had yet to escape.

Now here was this powerful, strong, *determined* man looming over her, wanting something from her that she didn't quite understand. It was hard for her to figure out.

And then, it was hard for her to even think.

The sheriff leaned down and pressed his lips to hers. For real this time. Not just a quick little brush like before.

18

KISSING HER AGAIN HAD BEEN THE BIGGEST mistake of his life. He knew that now. But damned if he wanted to stop. She'd left her hair loose for the day. He took advantage of that, burrowing his fingers under the soft auburn mass. She wasn't very experienced—that was evident in the tentative way she kissed him back—but she *was* kissing him back. That gave him hope.

He'd never been attracted to petite women before, but having this one trembling against him so small, so delicate, so...everything he wanted at the moment...

Did she realize that?

Her mouth opened beneath his, and he took

advantage. Nothing threatening, nothing over-whelming, nothing that would frighten her. He just wanted to taste her, to kiss her, and hold her. It had been a long while since he'd been this at-tracted to a woman. He didn't know where it was going to go, or even if he wanted to go anywhere. But the possibility did exist.

He forced himself to back away from her; she was inexperienced and vulnerable. He was nine years older than she was, and worlds' more experi-enced. World-weary even, in a way that *she* obvi-ously wasn't. And there were three children in the house. He wasn't about to take advantage of her now. Or at all. So he kissed her one more time and then pulled away. "Do you understand now?"

"I..." She stared up at him, her hands still spread across his chest. "Why did you do that?"

"Because I have been thinking of *nothing* else for days. Every time I see you, the desire to do that just gets stronger and stronger. I figured we better get it out of the way before we can tackle the problem that is your brother."

"He's not a problem. He's just a confused and hurting kid who went through a hard time." Fire went through her blue eyes. As he had expected it would. Joel cupped her cheeks with his fingers.

And brushed his lips against hers again. And then he kissed the flush in her cheeks before deliberately putting some space between them.

"Yes, he is. And he'll have to be dealt with. But there is also something between *us*, honey. So we'll deal with your brother first. Before anything else. Because no matter what he is messed up in, I don't want it to have anything to do with us. You and me."

"I hate to sound like a TV cliché, Sheriff, but there is no *us*. There is me, my *family*. That's all I have time for; that's all I want. And that's all that I'm going to do. My family, me. What do you really want from me? Or are you just trying to confuse me?"

He laughed. He couldn't help himself. His hands were still around her waist, and he used that to his advantage now; it was so easy to lift her. He'd wrestled bigger calves than this woman. He sat her back away from him. As much out of arm's reach as he possibly could. "I'm not going to search in here any longer. If need be, I'll deal with your brother separately. Then I will *deal* with you."

"Can't you send out a deputy? I'm not sure I want you here anymore. You're...too confusing. I'm not one to lie, *Joel*. You overwhelm me; I don't think I can deal with that right now. I've got too much on my plate. Surely you understand that?"

Yes, she did have too much on her plate. Too much for any one person, whether she shared it with those sisters of hers or not. Surely she realized that? He certainly did. But maybe by dealing with her brother, he could help ease her load. Just a little.

"*I* am the one responsible for keeping you safe. No deputy. Unless I absolutely have to. I'm not going to pressure you, Phoebe. We can take it as slow as you like. But when—*if*—you ever decide how you want to handle me, you just let me know. I'll be right here, waiting. Something to keep in mind." He ran a hand down her cheek lightly. Something about this woman made his hands itch to touch. Hell, they'd itched to touch her from the very beginning, hadn't they? "Something you have to consider. I'm going to get going now. Lock your doors behind me. Keep them locked until your father gets home. Promise me that."

19

It was early the next morning when she saw him again. His brother Matt—the *nice* one—had come and gone yesterday, taking the two geldings and giving them enough cash to pay the newest hospital bill looming over their heads and to give them enough for several months of groceries, barely.

When combined with the beef their father had had slaughtered, and the chickens in the backyard, the eggs from those chickens, and the vegetables she and her sisters put back each year, they would be ok for three months or so.

She and her sisters had spent a few hours over

the past few days trying to juggle the budget. They needed to find the money to fix the car that had inexplicably broken down on Perci's way home the night before and still have enough for their groceries. It was going to be a real tight squeeze.

They were going to delay some of the bills to stock up the pantry. As far as Phoebe was concerned, bills—they would always have, but they had *child* mouths to feed. And that was far more important than paying the hospital for the three days her mother was in a coma two years ago. They had been paying *that* bill close to two years now, and it was damned near beggaring them. She wasn't about to let it starve them, too—or let her father file bankruptcy as he'd suggested just after *his* heart attack eighteen months ago. Which had just added more bills to their pile.

The hospital would get paid. One day. But until then, her brothers needed to eat.

She and the twins headed into Masterson, both to get Perci's car to the mechanic—who'd agreed to take part of the repair bill in trade for some of her mohair yarn, thankfully—and to stock up on the groceries. Pan was off somewhere, cleaning extra houses to help with buying gasoline *for* those cars. It was a never-ending cycle, wasn't it?

It had been a while since she and Pip had been into town, other than her trip to the ER. It had been even longer since the three of them had been into town together—without the boys trailing behind them.

Perci treated them with her share of her paycheck to lunch in the Masterson Diner. They were just finishing up when the front door opened. Perci groaned—loud enough for even Phoebe to hear. Phoebe followed her sisters' gazes.

The sheriff of Masterson County and two of his equally handsome younger brothers stood in the doorway.

Pip took a French fry from Phoebe's plate. She used it to point to the trio of cowboys who had drawn attention when they'd entered. "Now *those* are the kind of men Mama warned us about. See how pretty they look? It just isn't fair."

Phoebe snickered, but she saw exactly what her sister meant. They eclipsed other men around them, didn't they? Long, lean, and handsome, all three. Made that brute Tom Rutherford and his pals look like thugs sitting there by the window.

"Mama also said *pretty is as pretty does*. That

doesn't leave much room for Dr. Masterson, I'm afraid. The guy is a total jerk."

"His brother seemed ok. He knows horses." And for Pip that mattered. Her sister was far more at home with the animals than she was real people.

Phoebe was no better. She preferred goats, after all. Goats were just so much easier to understand than men like the sheriff.

The sheriff who hadn't yet spotted them. He and his brothers stopped off at the counter to give their orders. It was the only chance she and her sisters had to escape.

Phoebe looked back at her sisters. Perci was already gathering their trash. Pip grabbed their bags.

"Hurry," Phoebe whispered. "I *don't* want to talk to him right now."

The Masterson brothers hadn't noticed them in the back booth yet. She just hoped they wouldn't until she and her sisters made their escape.

It didn't happen.

Because Tom Rutherford just couldn't resist being a total jerk on their way out.

The big man, equally as large as the sheriff,

stepped right into Phoebe's path at the very last minute.

She had nowhere to go to escape him and hit him in the chest dead on.

And Tom took advantage of it. He locked his arms around her and wouldn't let go. The jerk seemed to enjoy having her push away from him. He even dropped one hand down to her rear for just a half second. Damn him. He'd mostly left her and her sisters alone, but now...

"Well, look here. It's some of the *Tyler* sisters. Out from the pigs today? Where's that brother of yours? I have some...questions for him."

Rutherford's hands were tight on Phoebe's arms. She tried to pull away, but he was a bully and an ass—and strong with it. She forced herself to stand still, knowing the man would just enjoy her squirming more. His body was already hardening against her. Disgust threatened to have her lunch returning the hard way. "Let me go, Tom."

"*Let me go, Tom,* she says. Maybe...maybe I don't want to." His fingers tightened. His two friends stood, trapping her sisters between them. Phoebe glanced at Pip and Perci, seeing the fear on Pip's face. The fury on Perci's. Rutherford lifted her slightly. "So...which one are you again? Ah... the deaf one."

"Let me go!" All she had to do was call out. She knew they were already drawing attention their way. She half thought she recognized two of her cousins in the far corner of the diner.

Martin and Mike wouldn't let anything happen, surely.

And the sheriff...

Joel was in the diner, too. She forced herself to breathe and *think*. All she had to do was call out, and *Joel* would be right there.

A fact one of Rutherford's buddies pointed out. "Let her go, Tom. Sheriff's right over there. We don't need him butting in right now."

Rutherford squeezed her tightly. "I don't *want* to. It's been *two years* since I last held such a beautiful woman." He leaned down next to her left ear. "Can you hear me, little girl? I bet you're a real firecracker in the sack, aren't you? I can't wait to find out. I can guarantee you'll love it. I'll make you scream so loud..."

Perci took matters into her own hands. "Let her *go*, Rutherford. You're being a big prick. Are you overcompensating for the small one in your pants again?"

He shoved Phoebe away slightly, though he kept one hand on her. He turned on her younger sister, his arm raised back to strike.

And that was all it took.

No one hurt one of her siblings. No one. Phoebe reached out and bit him.

20

JOEL GLANCED UP AT THE SOUND OF A MAN yelling. The diner hushed immediately. One look at the small redheads near the doors and his heart started pounding.

Phoebe.

Joel was already moving.

Nate cursed beside him. "They've baited the bull with that one."

"I think she had a good reason," Matt said, putting his food down on the counter. "Rutherford has the smallest one by the arm, and I don't think she asked for him to touch her."

The *smallest one.* Damn it. "*Phoebe.*"

Rutherford's soda was unceremoniously

dumped over his large, blond head. Rutherford yelled the instant the soda struck him. "You *bitches!*"

Phoebe jumped between the big man and her sister, physically trying to block the man's attack.

And it was a definite attack. Rutherford lifted his hand to strike out at the much smaller women. One of his buddies stopped him just a fraction of a second before he struck Phoebe or her sister.

The entire diner was stunned. Joel jumped into action.

Nate was closer; when had his brother started moving?

Nate lifted the twin out of the way just as Joel reached Phoebe and pulled her toward safety. He nudged her toward the quieter twin, who wrapped her arms around Phoebe protectively. "Keep yourselves back."

Joel turned toward Rutherford. "Tom, what the hell are you doing?"

"Damned Tyler bitches assaulted me. That deaf bitch *bit* me for no good reason!"

"*Liar.* He had Phoebe and wouldn't let her go *first*," the fiery twin said from somewhere behind Nate's shoulder. Nate was keeping her back as best he could. "Look at her arms if you don't believe me!"

Joel did just that, fighting the instinct he had telling him to just plow his fist right into Rutherford's face.

Livid red marks covered Phoebe's pale skinny arms. One was even bleeding. "Phoebe, honey? Are you ok?"

"What the hell, Masterson? You're *fucking* her!" Rutherford said loudly enough for the entire diner to hear. Rutherford sneered at the three women. He reached out, almost grabbing little Pip's elbow. She cried out and twisted away, pulling Phoebe with her. "Or is it one of the other two?"

"You're stepping over the line real fast, Rutherford," Joel said. If he hadn't been wearing his badge, he would have already knocked the guy's teeth down his throat for the marks on Phoebe's soft skin.

Joel risked a glance at her. Big blue eyes watched him out of that too pale face. Terrified again. Her sisters were right there next to her, his brothers between them and the threat. Joel looked around the diner. Everyone was watching, no doubt about that.

And three strong men were standing near the back booth, dark expressions on their faces.

Oh, *hell*. Martin Tyler and two of his seven brothers. One thing about the troublemaking Tylers, they protected Tyler women. *Fiercely.* Martin looked about ready to do some serious damage.

Joel slipped a hand behind himself and nudged Phoebe and Pip a little closer to Matt. Just to be on the safe side. Things could go ugly real fast, and he didn't want them too near to the fight.

"Rutherford, I suggest you head on outside. Time to cool off." He looked at Phoebe's cousin, a big man with hair the same shade of auburn and eyes the same blue. Martin Tyler was ready to tear into someone. The man had one hell of a temper and an even worse right hook. Joel knew from personal experience. "Last thing you need is a brawl with the Tyler brothers right here, Tom. You know I'm not going to let anyone pound on anyone else. Keep the peace and all."

"You and what army, Sheriff?" Rutherford turned the full force of his anger on Joel. "Didn't realize the sheriff's office was in bed with the damned Tylers. Hope she's a good fuck, Masterson. She certainly looks like she would be. All that fire...would love to get my hands on her...just for an hour or two. Show her what a real man rides like. Her or her three sisters. I'm not particular about which piece of Tyler trash I screw. One Tyler slut is as good a lay as the others."

It took everything Joel had *not* to shove the man's nose back into his skull the hard way.

Even Nate and Matt looked ready to take a swing at Rutherford for that last insult. They'd been raised better than to let someone talk to a woman that way.

If he didn't act fast, Tom Rutherford was going to get the pounding he no doubt deserved. Possibly from Joel's own brothers.

21

Phoebe knew Tom Rutherford meant the hate-filled look he shot at her and the twins. It was only Joel, his brothers, and three of her cousins that kept the big brute from hurting one of them. "Sheriff...Joel...we don't want any trouble." Not for themselves, and not for him. He didn't need Tom Rutherford causing him trouble. Not like this. Tom was well-liked in the county. Joel was in a political position. She couldn't get him involved in her family's drama like this.

"Your sister dumped soda on me!"

"You had your hands on my sister. What was I supposed to do?" Perci was ready to jump right back in and defend. Like she always was. Joel's brother physically stopped her.

"Tell you what. I'm going to just pretend *nothing* happened today. That I *didn't* see you ready to hit women more than two hundred pounds smaller than you are, Tom. Going to forget that I see where that woman is going to have bruises because of you. Everything is just fine, and we're all happy. Tyler ladies, if you'll allow me to walk you to your car? Matt, can you grab our lunch? Nate, you can probably let that one go now."

Nate snorted. "Not so sure that's a great idea. She tends to go rabid when she's angry."

Phoebe had to admire the way Joel diffused the situation. He seemed good at it. And she wouldn't lie, having him there made her feel a little less intimidated. He kept one hot hand splayed over her back and his strong body between hers and Rutherford's. The scent of him surrounded her again.

For a moment she just wanted to breathe him in. Stay safe right where she was for a long while.

The man was dangerous to her sanity—that was for sure.

Perci and the doctor walked out behind them,

snapping at each other the whole way. Pip was behind, quiet as usual.

As soon as they were clear of prying eyes, Joel stopped walking and turned to her. Pip and Perci kept walking to where Pip's truck was parked.

Phoebe didn't know what to say. Rutherford had scared her. There had been a real hatred in his eyes when he'd looked at her, in his hands when he'd grabbed her. She shivered, and before she realized it, her hand tightened on his arm. "Thank you. Tom Rutherford hates all of us."

He brushed one hand down her bare arm. Rutherford's blunt fingernails had dug in. She would have little half-moon marks and bruises on her upper arms for a few days.

"Damn it. I should have arrested him."

"Well, I did bite him." And she was rather proud of herself for that.

"Still, he had no right. I should go back and—"

"And just make the situation worse? We just try to stay out of his way when we can. Except for Perci. She hates that the old sheriff blamed Phoenix for the wreck that killed Sadie Rutherford."

Joel's eyes showed his surprise. Phoebe understood. No one believed Phoenix *except* the Tylers. "He wasn't at fault?"

"Perci says he wasn't, and she was the only other person to survive. But the old sheriff blamed our family. There's a lot of that in this county. He seemed to have it out for my dad my whole life. I voted for you, just to not vote for him. But that was before I knew you. A lot of history in this county surrounding my family."

"*Not* with me. What are you doing in town so early? I was going to stop by later. Once I shook my brothers. They're like fleas at times."

"Perci's car needed to be fixed, and we are stocking up the pantry." It was warm out, but she was still chilled. But he was strong and warm and right there in front of her.

He looked around them quickly, then wrapped his hand around her neck under her loose fall of hair. Before she even realized what he had intended to do, he covered her mouth with his own. The kiss lasted less than a quarter of a minute, but when he pulled away, she just stared up at him like an idiot.

"I'll still be out tonight. I need to find your brother. Ask him a few questions."

"I haven't seen him in a while." She risked a

glance back toward the truck. Perci was busy arguing heatedly with the sheriff's doctor brother, but *Pip* was inside the truck, watching. Phoebe had no doubt that her quieter sister had seen everything. Pip usually did.

"I'll find him. In the meantime, I think your sisters are waiting. There's the third one now."

He touched her again, just a simple brush of his fingers down her arm. But that was all it took.

Sheriff Joel Masterson had twisted her all inside out, and she didn't have a clue how to deal with it.

She watched him walk away with two of his brothers, to join the third who'd appeared next to the parking lot—where Pan's little two-door was parked. She and the youngest Masterson brother looked deep in conversation. Phoebe considered catching a ride with Pan to avoid Pip and Perci, but her youngest sister just waved her away. She'd find out what Pan was doing with Levi Masterson later.

The twins were in the truck waiting when Phoebe finally opened the passenger door.

For once they were *both* silent. Finally, Perci spoke. It was always Perci who spoke, wasn't it?

"The sheriff *kissed* you. And you *let* him. Really kissed you."

"I don't think it's the first time he's kissed her either," Pip added. "I'd bet good money on it."

Phoebe looked out the window at the small town and tried to pretend her cheeks weren't red. "Shut up."

"He *has*. Maybe that's why he's been coming around so much. Not because of the bloody message but because of *her*," Pip said.

"Other than when he was berating her for being an idiot over not staying in the hospital that night, he was pretty damned sweet with her. Calling her *honey*, carrying her like he did. *Watching* her. And since then...well...guess we've been blind, Pip. Sheriff Masterson has a *crush* on our Phoebe."

"Stop it, you two. And just drive. The mechanic said to be there in an hour. We're past that, remember?" They needed Perci's car. "There's nothing between the sheriff and me. And there's *not* going to be. How could there be when I barely have two minutes to *myself* with this family, let alone time for a man like him? No, it's not going to happen. And the sooner *he* realizes that, the better."

Pip was silent for a long moment. "Maybe. But with the right man, would it really matter? Wouldn't he just kind of *fit?* Somehow just seem to *always* be there? Make you feel safe and loved... and not afraid?"

Perci picked up her train of thought like they often did to one another. "Won't it be *easy?* Mama always said it just felt right with Daddy."

"There is nothing *easy* about Joel Masterson. I don't see how there ever could be."

22

His brothers were staring at him when Joel returned to the diner after he'd made certain Phoebe and her sisters drove off in their truck safely. He looked at Nate. "You are going to have to quit arguing with that girl. It's starting to get ridiculous."

Nate snarled for a moment. He was the largest of the brothers and looked dog mean. Until someone got to know him and realized the tough exterior hid a heart full of compassion. It was why his brother had chosen medicine after all. Nate couldn't stand to see someone in pain. "She's a *Tyler*. That little demonstration should show it all."

"What it showed is that Tom Rutherford is an asshole. He left marks on Phoebe. She'll bruise. I'm still half tempted to book him on assault charges." The sight of the red marks on her skin burned right through him. Phoebe hadn't done a damned thing to hurt Tom Rutherford.

He hadn't forgotten the bloody message on the Tylers' back porch.

It was entirely possible Rutherford was responsible.

Joel lost his appetite for his burger and fries. He shoved them at his youngest brother just as Levi sat down next to him.

"So what did I miss? What happened with Rutherford?"

"Why were you with Pandora Tyler?" Joel shot back. Levi and the youngest sister hadn't been anywhere near the diner when Rutherford had happened. But they had been together, hadn't they?

"Oh. She answered the ad for a housekeeper we placed. I hired her. She's young but has experience *and* references. Best we're going to get for what we want to pay."

Nate cursed. "Damn it, I just can't escape the Tylers. And now one will be in our home?"

Joel took a swig of his soda. "Question is, why would any sane man *want* to escape women like that?"

23

JOEL PULLED INTO THE TYLER DRIVEWAY AT just a few minutes past five-thirty.

It was the first time since he'd started coming out there regularly that he'd managed to catch them *all* at home.

He was greeted on the front porch by the little boy with Phoebe's face and light reddish-blond hair. She'd said he was seven, hadn't she? And she'd been taking care of him for at least two years, longer. This kid was as close to being *her* child as was possible without her being his actual mother, wasn't he?

That thought overwhelmed Joel for a moment. Made him see what she'd flat out said earlier. Any man getting involved with Phoebe Tyler was taking on *all* of the Tylers. All of them. Something the man would have to consider very, very carefully. "Hey, Parker. How are you doing tonight?"

"Pip and Phoebe are making dinner." The boy stared at him out of those Tyler blue eyes. "Daddy and Pan and Perci are arguing."

"Oh?"

"Pan wants to go live on a horse ranch far away and clean house for a bunch of men instead of for us. I don't want her to go. Neither do Daddy and Perci. Phoebe says Pan has to do what Pan has to do. Pip says whatever makes Pan happy. Peter says they reached a stale...gate. I'm not sure what that means. Can I see your badge?"

"It's *stalemate*. It means two sides can't come to an agreement. Kind of like a tie in a game." Joel took off his badge and let the kid hold it for a minute. "My brother told me he offered her the job. She'd come live at our ranch. She'd cook and clean for *my brothers and me*. We're not all that far away. I'm on my way out there now."

"What's wrong with staying here and helping Phoebe with my brothers and me?"

"Nothing, I suppose."

"I don't want my sisters to ever leave. My

mommy did. In the car. She went to heaven that way."

"I know, buddy."

"Do you have a dog? I do. She's a border collie named Libby. I tried to ride her once. Phoebe said *no*. Said I couldn't ride the cows or the goats either." He grinned, looking very much like his oldest sister. So much so that Joel was a goner. The kid was awesome. "*Pip* taught me to ride Air Dancer instead. He's huge."

"Is he?"

"Uh-huh. He's Sky Dancer and Wind Dancer and Cloud Dancer's big brother." Parker picked up a stick and sword-fought an imaginary bad guy. "Why are you here? Are you going to take Phoebe away now? Put her in jail for kicking you?"

"Uh, no. Your sister had good reason to kick me. She thought she was protecting your brother."

"Phoenix is always causing trouble."

"So I've heard."

"I'm not going to cause trouble. I'm going to be a policeman. Then people will be afraid of *me* like Phoebe was afraid of that old sheriff. He was really mean to her once. And yelled at her, called her *stupid* because she couldn't hear him. And other mean names. *I* think *he* was stupid."

"Well, he's not the sheriff any longer. I am. People liked me better. And I'll never be mean to Phoebe. I like Phoebe, very much." Very, very much.

"Your brother is mean to my Perci."

"Is he?"

"She comes home crying sometimes. In her room. She doesn't know that I wake up every night when she comes home. I'm her brother." Big blue eyes again. "I'm supposed to protect her. So I wake up to make sure she comes home."

"I'll tell Nate to be really nice to your sister because you said so. How does that sound?"

The child nodded and took Joel's hand in his. "That will work. I think Phoebe likes you."

"Do you?"

"Her cheeks turn red like her hair when she talks about you." Parker led him up the porch steps, where Patton was napping in a hammock, the old border collie curled around him. How had the dog even gotten up there? "Did she really bite the bad guy today? Before you rescued her?"

"Yes. She did. Phoebe can take care of herself just fine. But I'm going to be there to help her when she needs me. Is that ok with you?"

Parker was quiet for a moment. Then he

nodded solemnly. "I suppose so. As long as you promise not to take her away."

PHOEBE WAS LISTENING AS BEST SHE COULD TO the argument behind her and missed the sound of the back door opening up into the kitchen. It was only when a dark shadow fell over the pot of pasta she was stirring that she looked up.

Right into Joel's dark-green eyes. "Joel!"

The room immediately quieted. She looked around to make sure no one was whispering too low for her to hear. Her father was still sitting in his chair at the head of the table. Pan was pacing in front of him, agitated and red-faced.

Phoebe wasn't too thrilled with the idea of her youngest sister going to live on the *Masterson* ranch, of all places. But she had to admit the salary Levi Masterson was offering was far more than what Pan was bringing in cleaning for various clients during the day. And she'd still have time to do her clerical work online. She'd even mentioned Levi Masterson telling her she could help *him* with records for an additional fee.

Room and board and *health insurance* were

also included. Pan would actually come out ahead by taking the job. It would be one less mouth for them to feed here. Of course, it would also mean one less pair of hands to help around here.

But Pan had to do what Pan had to do. Her sister deserved to make her own path, her own future, without being tied down here. Phoebe knew it was coming for a while. Pan needed more than the ranch could give her. She needed to discover what *she* was capable of accomplishing.

They weren't going to stand in her way. What kind of family would they be then?

Perci just didn't want Pan going near Nate Masterson, let alone working for him. Phoebe understood that, too.

Their father didn't want his youngest daughter living with four single men, alone on their ranch with just them and a bunch of male hired hands. He thought it was just asking for trouble.

Now *that* was something Phoebe could agree on.

Joel had probably picked a very poor time to come by.

Parker was clinging to his hand, looking up at the tall man in the white Stetson with a bit of hero-worship in his eyes. "I found the sheriff! He's not here to take you away or nothing, Phoebe. He promised. Can he stay for dinner, please?"

"Urgh! Another *Masterson*. They're everywhere I turn lately!" Perci shot him a glare as if he'd caused all of her problems with the doctor brother.

"Actually, I think you Tylers outnumber us Mastersons two-to-one, Perci. But if you'd like, I'll happily help you lock Nate in the woodshed for a few hours. Could put a duck in there with him. He's terrified of ducks, you know. Comes from the time Matt and I may have set an attack duck on him for pestering Levi."

"Quack, quack. I'm getting a pet duck." An evil glare entered her sister's eyes. Then Perci sobered. "We don't like this job offer."

Joel held up his hands. "Hey, not my thing. I will tell you this: my brother Levi takes running his ranch—all of our properties—very seriously. He didn't pick your sister on a whim. He's a professional. And he'll make sure your sister is just fine. Hell, so will I. She'll have her own apartment even. We're not ogres—well, Matt, Levi, and I aren't. Nate was found under a rock." Joel looked at her father. "Your daughter will be safe with us. I can promise you that."

"She's a grown woman, I guess. Time to let her —to let them *all*—make their own decisions. I have held them back these past two years, and I know that. But enough is enough. Pandora, baby girl, you have my blessing. And the door is always open if you need to come home."

Pan hugged their father.

Phoebe struggled not to cry.

It seemed like her family was splintering off right in front of her, almost overnight. First, Phoenix, now Pan. Who was going to be next?

24

After dinner, Joel brought up the real reason he'd stopped by. Phoebe's father listened quietly. "He's still up at the cabin. And the bridge up there is flooded out right now."

"Only way up there is by horseback," Pip said. "If you left now, you could get up there and back by nightfall. But it'll be pushing it."

Joel couldn't put it off any longer, and he knew it. "I need to see him tonight. Rule him out as a suspect before the state police get involved. It's better he deal with me than with them."

Phil looked at his four daughters, one by one. "Someone will have to take you up there. It's not exactly a well-known path."

"I'm out. Sorry, it's the whole anti-Masterson thing I have going on." Perci sent him a smirk. "But don't worry. I kind of half like you, Sheriff. You're not half bad."

"Gee, thanks, Persephone. I'll be sure to give your love and best to my brother when I get home." Sure enough, a sneer hit her beautiful face. Joel was starting to understand—the two were attracted to each other and pissed off about it.

"I can't. I'm packing tonight. I told Levi that I'd be there first thing in the morning. Can't be late because I've been out in the woods with the boss's brother."

Joel looked at little Pip, the quietest sister. She just shook her head. "I have to be in town tomorrow to pick up a horse by nine a.m. We're going to be boarding her, and I haven't gotten her stall ready yet."

He fought back a smile, as her sisters seemed to be conspiring to give him exactly what he wanted. He looked at the eldest sister. Her eyes were big and wide, and she knew exactly what he was about to ask. Joel held out a hand to her. "Phoebe, honey?"

She visibly swallowed and looked at her father. "Daddy?"

"I'm leaving first light myself, sweetie. You know I can't miss my plane. Too much hinges on convincing that Finley Creek rancher to let me use his bull as a stud. A W. Deane line in our cattle will make a huge difference..."

Phoebe looked back at him. "We'll head up now. Then...get back here as quickly as possible."

"Of course." Joel was looking forward to having the woman to himself for more than half an hour at a time. Yes, it might be only a ninety-minute horse ride or so, but it was just the two of them. Alone.

He couldn't wait to head up the mountain.

AFTER ABOUT THE FIRST FIFTEEN MINUTES OF riding toward the back corner of her family's property, Phoebe started to relax. Started to forget how the man had her all tied up in knots and began to enjoy the feel of the horse beneath her and experience the beautiful world around her.

The man. Whenever she looked at *him* a thrill of something very close to hunger and anticipation went through her.

She did not know this man, but she wanted to.

Wanted to be with him, figure out just why *he* wanted to be with her. And what she wanted to give him.

Something her sisters had said had struck her in the diner parking lot. *When it was right, it should be easy.*

But that didn't seem to describe what she felt when with this man.

There was nothing *easy* about being with the sheriff of Masterson County, was there? It was all emotion—anger, fear, yes. But it was also excitement, anticipation, and—she wasn't going to hide it from herself—*lust*. Something more than that.

Had she ever been quite this attracted to a man before?

She didn't think she ever had. There had been boys in her life, her teen years, even her early twenties. But nothing like what she felt for this man.

Phoebe didn't know what she wanted to do about that.

To be honest, it would probably come to nothing. She couldn't see *him* making such a drastic change in his life to make room for the Tylers. It just wasn't about to happen.

But did that mean she couldn't make a small space in *her* life, did it?

She didn't want to spend the rest of her life alone. She wanted to *experience* everything life had to offer. And that included love.

Or even just this small part of it.

As they continued up the mountain, Phoebe tried to figure out just exactly what it was she wanted from him.

25

THE CABIN WAITED UP JUST AHEAD. THANK God. They'd make it before the approaching storms hit. The weather reports had mentioned nothing of a storm. They'd been wrong. Joel kept his horse on the small path, just behind hers. The woman was one hell of a rider; no one could miss that.

They reached the front of the small cabin that had to be close to one hundred fifty years old, and she called her brother's name. No response. She called again.

"His truck isn't here." She turned toward Joel and shaded her eyes from the setting sun. "He may be in town. Something with the school."

"Then we wait." He dismounted then reached up for her. She hesitated a moment, then leaned into his hands.

She was wary of him now, aware in a way she hadn't been before. He wasn't sure if that was a good thing or not. He didn't want to rush her at all. But it had been a damned long time since he'd felt an attraction to a woman this strongly.

"The storm?"

He shook his head. There was no way they were going to be able to ride back down the mountain tonight. Their best bet would be to stable the horses in the small lean-to behind the cabin and head back at first light.

And take that time to really get through to that idiot younger brother of hers. Find the answers he needed. "Honey, that storm is coming up on us a little too fast for comfort. We will never make it back to your place—unless your brother gets back with his truck. Which is a big *if.* The Stoddard Bridge was washed out last time I rode through there."

She paled. "We may be surrounded by floodwaters? I need to get home to the boys."

"Honey, it just isn't going to happen."

"I need to call my sisters."

He pulled his phone free and checked the display. He had two bars, which was better than most areas of the county. Phoebe didn't have a phone at all, something he didn't understand. With all those boys she was practically raising, she needed a cell phone. He handed it to her. "Call your father. Let him know that you're safe."

"Am I? Somehow I wonder."

"Well, you can tell him you're safe...unless you choose not to be."

He listened as she called her father and gave very clear instructions to everyone in the house. It took a while to convince her sisters that she didn't need them to ride up to the cabin and rescue her.

He appreciated the irony in that. Her voice softened when she spoke to the youngest boy. Joel bit back a smile as she told him to make sure he read a chapter in his reading book before bed.

The Tylers didn't have much material wealth, but they had each other. And that made them very fortunate.

He had his mother, Nate, Levi, and Matt, and that was about it. There were cousins sprinkled throughout the county. He was close to his brothers—they were his closest friends—but Phoebe's family took that to another level. The degree to which they depended on each other spoke volumes. She disconnected then handed the phone back to him.

"I don't remember the last time I was away from the boys for a full night. Probably back before Parker was born. I came back home from college when Mom was pregnant. She was so sick with him, and after he was born..."

He got it. She'd probably taken a lot on herself. She would have been around what? Eighteen? Which meant her younger sisters would have been sixteen and fourteen or so. An awful lot of responsibility for so young. "Did you go back?"

"Hmmm? No. I finished a few classes online, but...well...things happened. Besides, I'm doing what I love to do. My weaving...well, there aren't a whole lot of classes for weavers, are there?" She smiled, a light of joy in those blue eyes of hers.

And at *that* moment, he got it. *Truly* understood it. Phoebe was *happy*. All her family's problems aside, she took joy from what she did each day.

He wasn't so certain he could say the same thing.

Joel looked at her and *knew* exactly how to change that, to *feel* that joy again.

26

Nate had made the decision to call in every member of the on-call staff the instant the flood warnings came in. It was better to be prepared than to send his small hospital into a code-black situation. It wasn't just floods they were predicting, but severe storms.

Persephone was the first one to arrive. No surprise. She took one look at him. "Hey, Masterson, your brother took my sister up into the mountains an hour ago."

"Why?"

"Looking for *my* brother." There was snark in her words, like always. But he also heard the concern. "I'm not certain they'll make it back before all hell breaks."

Nate pulled out his cell. He dialed his brother quickly. It was a two-minute conversation, and it reassured him. "They're going to stay put up in that cabin. The river was rising when they crossed."

She nodded and put her coat—why hadn't he ever noticed before how threadbare it actually was?—in her locker. "Good. That river has washed out before."

"Joel's not stupid. He'll keep your sister safe."

"But who's going to keep her safe from him? He's getting a little randy with my sister."

"Joel's always been the bravest of our lot."

"Ha ha. Like Phoebe could ever hurt a Masterson."

"Oh, I'm sure a woman like your sister"—like *you*, he thought—"could tear a man into pieces with just one look."

"Hey, we try."

"Get out there. I have a feeling tonight is going to be a rough one."

27

PHOENIX WASN'T GOING TO MAKE IT BACK before the storm. Phoebe didn't know how she felt about that. It wasn't something she'd intended or expected. It wasn't supposed to rain *or* storm today. She'd double-checked just that morning. Apparently, the weather report had been wrong. Dead wrong.

She heard the thunder, even with her limited hearing. It was going to be a bad one. She led the way to the lean-to, and they made quick work of caring for Sky Dancer and Prancer, the gelding the sheriff had borrowed. The horses would be warm and dry and safe for the night.

The torrential rain had started by the time they were finished.

Phoebe was soaked almost clear through just on the ten feet between the opening of the lean-to and the cabin's front door.

Joel hadn't fared any better.

He took off his white hat and tossed it on the small table. Phoenix had made an effort to keep the place clean at least. The dishes had been washed, the bed made, and everything was neat.

The bed dominated the room, dwarfing the single chair that sat by the small woodstove. Phoebe shivered.

They were there for the rest of the night, weren't they? And *something* had changed between them.

Unless Phoenix came. "My brother isn't going to be here?"

He stared at her for a long moment, then shook his head. The look of fire in his eyes had her shivering again. And it wasn't from her drenched clothes.

Which were dripping all over the hardwood floor.

As were his.

And there was no way he'd be able to fit into any of Phoenix's clothes.

"There's..." She cleared her throat and tried again. "There's a bathroom through there. I...there might be some of my brother's clothes that you can...that'll stretch...I mean...oh, hell. I'll just...get changed."

He stepped closer. One hand rose, and he flicked open the top button of her shirt. And then the next. "I can help."

Phoebe stood there, staring up at him, wondering what in the world she should do next. Wondering what it was that she *wanted* to do.

He undid the third button and then a fourth. "You're soaked."

"Yes." She couldn't stop shivering. She needed to get out of her wet clothes. She needed...

"Tell me. Yes or no. If it's yes, this shirt is coming off by *my* hands. If no...I'll go back outside until you're changed."

This was crazy. She'd known this man all of *two* weeks.

Two weeks wasn't long enough to make these kinds of choices, kinds of decisions, was it?

"Phoebe?"

His hand was so warm on her, even though he

wasn't actually *touching* her at the moment. He could. All he had to do was shift his hand just half an inch, and he could touch her. Damn, she felt his heat.

He could touch her.

In a way she hadn't been touched in a very long time.

"I...I can't...*won't* do more than this." Her resolve firmed, and when he tried to step away, she took the decision for herself. She slipped her hands over that strong, broad, *perfect* chest and unflicked one button. And then another. A third. A fourth. If she shifted her hands, either way, she could touch him the way *she* wanted to. "I can't do promises, Sheriff. I am a Tyler, and we keep our word on everything. Which means we don't make promises we don't know if we can keep. You need to understand that. So if you want more than that, I can't do it."

"I don't need promises. What I need is to taste you. Hold you. If all you can give me is a little while, then...I'm a big boy. I can deal with that." His fingers slipped to her shoulders. Her shirt fell from her arms, his clever hands making nothing of the remaining buttons. She stood there in the plain, white cotton bra she'd slipped on that morning after her shower. Plain, white cotton, faded clothes, worn jeans. The *need* he had for her.

He didn't seem to even notice. All she saw in his eyes was the hunger.

That was enough for her.

Phoebe reached for him.

28

THERE WAS AN INNOCENCE ABOUT PHOEBE. OF a kind he hadn't had in a very long time. Her hands were a little hesitant, and he wondered if it was because of nerves or unfamiliarity or because she just didn't know what she liked. What she wanted from him.

He wouldn't say he was jaded when it came to sex, but he'd definitely been around a time or two. Thought he'd done just about all of it in his thirty-five years. But with *her,* it all felt new.

Joel wrapped his arms around her and pulled her off her feet. "Wrap your legs around me."

"My jeans...my boots...they'll ruin the bed. Phoenix will ask questions."

He'd forgotten they still had their clothes on, hadn't he? Joel swore. "Let's get them off, sweetheart. Let's just get them off."

He didn't know whose hand unsnapped her jeans, but within seconds he was peeling wet denim down her legs. They tangled on her boots.

He made short work of them, too.

And then it was his turn.

Joel scooped her up again until they were chest to chest. Her eyes were wide and so blue he was drowning. Her lips trembled.

He had to taste.

So he did.

His hands, his mouth—he couldn't get enough of her. Joel forced himself not to rush. To remember that she wasn't as experienced, that he didn't want to frighten or overwhelm. That if this was all they were ever going to have together he wanted it to be perfect...*for her*.

He did his damnedest to make it that way.

29

NATE KNEW CALLING IN THE RESERVES HAD been a damned good idea. They'd had seventeen people get caught in the floods. People who should have known better. Floods happened in this part of the state all the damned time. People should know how to handle themselves in all sorts of weather situations. Wyoming was a flood-prone state.

The pneumatic doors slid open, and a pair of first responders rolled a young man in near first light the next morning. Unconscious. Nate, pulling a fill-in duty in the ER himself, stepped to the man's side. "Identification?"

"Phoenix Tyler. Nineteen. Found walking along Stoddard highway before he collapsed.

Need to call the sheriff's department. Someone worked the boy over good."

"Phoenix?" Nate leaned over him. "Hey, Phoenix. You're at the hospital. Perci's in one of the exam rooms. You're going to be ok."

Tiff, the head night nurse, heard him. "Hey, boss. Perci's clocking out now. She's hit the max sixty hours this week. She can't work anymore tonight."

"Page her. This is her younger brother."

The kid's hand shot up, and he wrapped his fingers around Nate's arm. Blue eyes opened. The kid ripped the mask off his bruised face. "Keep her *here!*"

"What happened to you? Who hurt you?"

"Tom...Rutherford. He says he's going to kill my sisters. One by one. Revenge for his wife. Tell Sheriff...planted pot...*our* ranch...to cause trouble for *us*. Don't let Perci out of your sight." The kid slid back into unconsciousness.

Nate went to work. Just as Perci jerked the curtain open and stepped into the exam room. She cried out, seeing her little brother.

Nate grabbed her arm, quickly. "Go! Call your father and your sisters. Warn them to keep themselves behind locked doors. Tom Rutherford did this. And your brother says he's going after you girls. Go. Call. He's going to be ok. I've got him."

And as soon as he had Phoenix taken care of, Nate was going to call his own brother. Tell him to watch his back up there.

30

NATE'S EYES LANDED ON JOEL'S SUV THE moment they pulled into the Tylers' front drive too close to noon the next morning. He'd been unable to reach his brother on Joel's cell. And thanks to the flooding, he hadn't been able to go look for him.

Neither had Levi or Matt, who'd been called in as reservists with the fire-and-rescue teams. But they'd kept trying. And now they were there to find their brother. Period.

Perci had called her father, but the older man had already taken off to Texas and was midflight. It was going to take him time to get back.

Perci had been safe at the hospital at her brother's side—until she'd snuck out a few hours ago and driven home. That woman was far too impulsive for her own good.

Joel's SUV stood out clearly amid the ramshackle old ranch house and broken walkway.

Ok, so they'd found his brother's Denali. Now, where was his brother? He climbed out of the truck and called for *her*. She should be around here somewhere.

The front door opened, and a beautiful redhead stepped out. But it wasn't the one he was expecting. This one's hair was too light. It must be his new housekeeper then.

He'd never expected to be greeted by a rifle, though. The young woman—what had his brother said, twenty-two?—stared at them for a long moment. The rifle was still gripped in her hands.

"We're looking for Joel, honey. You know where he is?" Levi asked. Nate's younger brother stepped up on the porch quickly and took the gun from her hands gently.

She shivered, almost uncontrollably. Nate had seen the after-effects of adrenaline before. "Joel and Phoebe took off up the mountain last night to find Phoenix. But he's at the hospital."

"I spoke with him myself," Nate said. He still wasn't certain he believed the boy's ramblings.

They were just a bit too farfetched. "Around eight. Just before the storms hit."

"And then we found an hour ago...after Perci got home...we found another message on the porch *after* Perci got home." She waved the men around the back of the house. Nate and his brothers followed her quickly.

Die, bitches, you're all going to die. Starting with the deaf one.

The threat was written bigger this time than the last one. And it was painted on the side of Persephone's little compact car. A stake of some sort had been driven through the windshield—right into the driver's seat.

"Where're your sisters?" Nate asked quickly. Persephone should have been out there next to her car, spitting mad. That she wasn't told its own story.

"They went up the mountain to find Phoebe and Joel right after we found this. In case whoever did that goes after Phoebe *now*."

"They're up there now?" Matt asked.

The girl nodded. "Yes. They took their guns."

Matt and his brothers shared a significant look. They needed horses, and fast. Matt was one hell of a decent tracker; they'd find those girls somehow.

In the meantime...

"Levi, you stay here with Pan and the kids." His brother was a damned good shot. Joel had made sure they all three were. He'd keep those kids and Pan safe.

"I've already called my cousins. Help will be here as fast as they can get here," Perci's little sister said.

"Stay inside," Matt ordered. "We're going to borrow a few horses."

"Just...hurry. We can't reach Joel on his phone, and Phoebe doesn't have one. They have no idea someone could be out there after them right now."

31

PHOEBE WAS JERKED AWAKE WHEN HARD hands yanked her out of Joel's arms. She screamed then looked up into Tom Rutherford's leering face. His lips moved into a sneer, but without her hearing aid, she couldn't make out what he'd said. She'd never been particularly good at reading lips.

She kicked out with her legs, still screaming.

Phoebe looked around, searching frantically for Joel. Where was he? He wouldn't leave her alone like this.

She found him bound on the floor, unconscious. What was going on? Why were they here?

Rutherford's brother was there, glaring at her from watery, red-rimmed eyes. Why was he there?

She kept fighting until Tom reached out and clubbed her across the left ear.

She fell to the floor.

His brother lifted her up, running one hand crudely over her chest. She closed her eyes and tried to *think*. To figure out what she was supposed to do now.

The men dragged her from the cabin. The harsh stones and twigs that littered the ground tore into her bare feet and slashed against the skin of her legs left exposed by the thin gym shorts she'd borrowed from her brother's drawers and dressed in after she and Joel had finished loving one another.

Joel.

Was he dead?

She froze beneath the men's hurtful hands for a long moment.

Until the cabin door opened and a long tall man rushed out.

JOEL HEARD HER SCREAM, AND THAT WAS ALL the incentive he needed. The assholes hadn't tied his hands properly, using trash-bag zip ties instead of actual law enforcement flex-cuffs. Flex-cuffs had tiny metal tabs that prevented them from being slipped open.

Not so with commercial ties. He popped the plastic around his wrists relatively easily. Joel barreled out the door, praying those assholes didn't just shoot him and get it over with.

They were too busy with Phoebe to worry about him.

Arguing over Phoebe.

Joel took the advantage he had and flew toward the bigger threat. Tom Rutherford went down. Joel yelled for Phoebe to run.

She obviously didn't hear him.

Her hearing aid. She didn't have it. Just how vulnerable that made her hit him in the gut—just seconds before Rutherford's fist slammed into him.

They rolled a few times, two large men, equally strong, equally determined. Joel wasn't about to lose, not with Phoebe right there.

She was struggling with the brother, but it was a losing battle. She was so damned small...

Joel slammed Rutherford to the ground and got lucky. Tom's head slammed into a rock. It wasn't enough to knock the man out, but it stunned him enough for Joel to jump to his feet and turn on Tom's younger brother, John.

The guy was smaller than Tom and had a history of drug abuse. And he'd always been a coward. To have a man Joel's size barreling down on him had him letting go of Phoebe and backing up quickly. Joel didn't give him a chance to escape—he slammed his fist into John's face, hearing the bones crack from the force.

He grabbed Phoebe by the arms and turned her to look at him. "Run!"

He made sure she understood, and he pointed down the mountain. "Go!"

She took off.

Just as Tom dove at Joel from the side.

32

PHOEBE TOOK OFF, JUST LIKE HE'D TOLD HER. She didn't have on her boots, but she didn't let that stop her. At first, she thought Joel was right behind her. It was only after she'd been running for a few minutes that she realized he wasn't.

She turned.

The man was gone. She couldn't see any signs of him or the Rutherfords.

And she wasn't about to let him face two armed men alone.

Phoebe turned back.

She knew every path that led to that cabin, having been hiking this side of the mountain her entire life. It took her no time at all to get behind the cabin and into the lean-to.

After that it was a simple matter of slipping back inside the cabin. She grabbed her boots and her hearing aid quickly. Within seconds she could hear again.

The sounds of a gunshot brought her running.

In time to see Joel go down as red spread over his broad chest. Tom Rutherford turned.

And looked straight at her. He'd already seen her. It didn't matter—she couldn't leave him. No matter what happened. Phoebe ran toward Joel and fell to her knees next to him. "Joel!"

"Phoebe, get out of here. Get back down the mountain to your family." Joel struggled to his feet. "Go, honey! Now! Get to your family, and get to my brothers. They'll keep you all safe!"

Just as Rutherford grabbed Phoebe from behind. "Well, look who came back. Ready for a real man now, sugar? You and I are going to go back in that cabin of your brother's and have a little fun."

"No!" Phoebe did the one thing she could. She jammed her knee straight into his groin and clawed for his eyes.

"Run, Phoebe! Go! I'll be right behind you!"

This time she didn't hesitate. Phoebe ran.

Rutherford was only steps behind her.

She wasn't about to lead a gun-carrying bastard down to her family, even if she did make it the hours it would take to hike back down to the house. Instead of turning south toward her family, Phoebe turned north.

Toward the mountains and cliffs that had overlooked her family home since the very beginning.

33

JOEL PULLED HIMSELF TO HIS FEET AND followed. Rutherford was damned fast on his feet. But so was Phoebe.

And she knew this area far better than Rutherford.

What was Rutherford doing on the Tyler property in the first place?

The Rutherfords yelled, cursing at Phoebe. Joel kept going as they approached the edge of the small creek that he and Phoebe had crossed the night before.

Floodwaters had swelled it overnight. It was now four times as wide as it had been and at least three feet deeper. And the rapids raged. It might not have been overly deep but it was damned dangerous for anyone foolish enough to fall in it.

Phoebe didn't even attempt to cross. Instead, she climbed the incline of the small hill where they'd stopped the night before to call her sisters. The waters rushed beneath the ten-foot cliff directly below. She'd kept climbing.

The three men were right behind her.

Rutherford grabbed for her.

And almost had her.

Joel was too damned far away to help her.

PHOEBE KEPT FIGHTING. IF SHE COULD GET TO the back highway that formed the southern boundary of her family's ranch, there was a US Forestry facility a mile up the road. It was often staffed with armed rangers. They could help, could call for backup. There was a high likelihood that *Joel* would know some of them.

It was the only thing she could think of.

She tripped, fell hard to the ground. Her arm cracked against a rock, and fierce pain shot through her.

Hard male hands grabbed her. One around her waist, the other tangled in her hair.

He jerked her to the ground. Phoebe screamed and fought. She grabbed a handful of dirt and flung it into the man's face.

The smaller Rutherford rolled off her and yelled out.

Phoebe scrambled to her feet, just as Tom grabbed her T-shirt.

He yanked her behind him, up the rocky hill until they were a good ways up the cliffs and the raging water was more than twenty feet below. Joel called out, and Phoebe turned to see him struggling with John. The smaller man grabbed a branch and swung, connecting with Joel's skull.

Joel went down and did not get back up again.

Joel. Phoebe screamed again as agonizing fear and grief rushed through her. She yanked away again and ran back down the hill toward him. The Rutherford brothers were far too close. Tom lashed out. The back of his hand connected with her cheek, and then she was falling. In that instant, Phoebe knew she was probably going to die. She screamed, even as she struck the surface of the floodwaters.

And then it was all she could do to hold on.

34

NATE TURNED HIS BORROWED HORSE—A damned fine horse—toward the screaming. It had been *women*. And chances were good that it had been Tylers.

Damn those Tylers and their propensity for finding trouble.

When he had her back safely, he was going to give Persephone Tyler a good tongue-lashing for this latest bit of stupidity. She should have called the sheriff's office, the state police, anyone, before heading up the mountain herself. Hell, it was his brother out there, too. She should have just called *him*. It would have had the same results, wouldn't it?

"There!" Matt pointed and shouted. Nate followed where his brother indicated.

A flash of red and white floated beneath them, smack in the midst of the raging floods. He couldn't tell which Tyler it was, but it didn't matter. He knew.

He'd seen Phoebe's fall into the waters just moments before.

But Phoebe was too far away for him and Matt to do much good. They couldn't even dive in after her. The water would push her just that much farther ahead of them. "Come on!"

The only choice they really had was to get ahead of her and hope...

Nate rounded the bend in the overflowing river and entered a small clearing. That's when another flash of red caught his eye. When he noticed the two beautiful horses.

The two small women braving the waters to reach their sister.

He cursed. What in the hell were they doing? It would never work.

Two one-hundred-ten-pound girls would *never* be strong enough to fight a raging river.

"They've at least got themselves tied off, Nate!" Matt yelled. He spurred his own horse on, insisting the animal brave the shallowest part of the flood waters. They *had* to get across. It was Phoebe's only chance. Hell, it might be the only chance all three of those girls had.

Nate looked for Phoebe again. Somehow she'd managed to grab on to a tree that had caught on a rock near the bank.

And one of those damned twins was *swimming* out toward her.

Nate forced his horse to cross the waters.

35

PHOEBE DID HER BEST TO SWIM TOWARD shore, but she was tiring. And her arms were hurting. She didn't know how much longer she could keep going. She'd lost her hearing aid somewhere—she couldn't even *hear* the rush of the water around her.

Then movement on the banks caught her attention. The water pulled her under, but she fought her way to the surface. She looked back toward the shore. The water slammed her into something, and she went under again, grabbing, grasping for anything she could.

Her hands went around a tree root as if by a miracle. If she could just hold on a little longer...

she could pull herself along the tree trunk toward the shore. If the tree just stayed jammed up against the rocks that jutted above the water...if the rocks weren't too slippery.

Phoebe wasn't going to give up.

Her sisters couldn't really be there, could they? Pip, the strongest swimmer in their family, was swimming toward her with a look of determination on her face.

Phoebe forced herself to hold on to the log as tightly as she could. She didn't even dare reach out to her little sister.

If the log broke free, it could snap back and hit her—or yank Pip under the waters completely. Pip yelled something, but there was no way. Phoebe shook her head quickly. Pip yelled again.

And then her sister was right there next to her. Reaching.

Phoebe refused to let go. She would pull her sister down under the water if she tried to take Pip's hand. The pressure of the river would kill them both. "No! Go back, Pip! Go back!"

But Pip was the stubbornest of her siblings by far. She held up her hand, and that's when Phoebe saw it.

Pip had a rope tied around herself. If it got caught on something, Pip wouldn't stand a chance.

Phoebe dared to look past her sister toward the bank. And there the other twin was, *Perci*. Perci was tied off to a tree that jutted out of the water near the shore, holding on to the rope that was tied to Pip.

It wouldn't *work*. There was no way Perci would ever be strong enough to pull them *both* out. Ever. Phoebe wasn't even certain Perci could pull *Pip* out against the raging current.

Pip got right in Phoebe's face, so close Phoebe couldn't miss what she said. "Go! I have the rope! Go first. Then help pull me back!"

Pip signed with one hand, making sure Phoebe couldn't misunderstand.

The force of the water threatened to yank Pip away, but her sister wrapped her arm around Phoebe and refused to budge.

No matter what.

Pip wasn't about to leave Phoebe out there. Any more than Pip would her.

Pip moved past her, grabbed the log herself.

The longer they argued, the more strength *Perci* was going to exert. If Phoebe made it back to shore, she and Perci could pull Pip. Pip, who had the rope.

The rope was *Phoebe's* only chance at all. There was no other way she could make it to shore.

If she let go, she was as good as dead.

Which meant so was Pip.

Phoebe forced herself to inch back up the rope, toward Perci, her injured arm protesting all the way.

36

NATE JUMPED OFF THE HORSE AND RAN, THE instant they were clear of the river crossing. He yelled Perci's name, telling her to just keep holding on, as more shouts came from the cliff more than forty feet above them. This part of the flooded river flowed through rocks taller than a four-story building. Phoebe was damned lucky she had gone over the edge south of there. If she'd been down here, she would have been killed instantly.

He scrambled over the loose rocks toward the woman trying in vain to hold on to the ones she loved.

Perci looked up at him, an expression of such stark terror on her face. The terror was immediately replaced by sheer relief the instant she recognized him. Such hope...such trust. Damn her. "I can't hold the rope much longer. I can't pull them. I can't."

"We can!" Nate wrapped his arms around her and started to pull. Matt did something even riskier. He went in at the water's edge, bracing himself behind a large boulder, and grabbed the rope with both hands. Matt started tugging even more strongly.

They were getting those girls out of the water, no matter what.

And then they were going to go find Joel.

37

JOEL HAD A MASSIVE HEADACHE, BUT HE DOVE at Tom Rutherford as the man aimed the rifle over the cliff's edge, knocking the man aside before he could squeeze off another round. Phoebe had to be down there somewhere. Why else would the man be shooting down that way?

Phoebe.

He had to find her. Joel didn't have time to screw around with Tom Rutherford.

Joel grabbed for the rifle, and his hand connected. He drove his elbow into Rutherford's nose as hard as he could. Rutherford might be a big sonofabitch, but so was Joel.

And he had a hell of a lot more incentive to win.

Rutherford lurched back. His momentum was enough to break Joel's hold on the rifle.

Rutherford swung out and clubbed Joel across the face with the grip, cursing. Joel went down.

Instead of coming at Joel, Rutherford went to the side of the cliffs again. He aimed the rifle at whatever was down there. "Damned Tylers ruining everything! Should have killed them off one by one before now!"

Joel lunged to his feet and knocked into the bigger man just as Rutherford shot off another round.

The two men went down.

Rutherford was too close to the edge. Rocks crumbled beneath him.

Somehow the bastard held on.

It was all Joel could do to keep the man from sending him catapulting over the side of the ledge.

Rutherford grabbed a handful of rock and dirt and jammed it in the direction of the still bleeding hole on Joel's chest. Rutherford bucked Joel off of him and charged.

Joel kept fighting. What other choice did he have? Phoebe needed him.

The two men rolled, each one dominating at some point or another. Until Joel realized they were so close to the damned edge.

Then he focused not on subduing Rutherford, but on getting free of the man's hold. Before Rutherford killed them both.

Finally, he got lucky.

Two inches from the edge.

Someone yelled out below him. A woman. *Phoebe.*

Joel did the only thing he could.

He pulled back his arm and drove his fist into Rutherford's face.

The other man screamed as he fell over the ledge to the river forty feet below.

And then Joel was at the edge, searching.

For *her.*

38

MATT WRAPPED HIS ARMS AROUND PHOEBE and lifted her out of the water toward the shore. Nate's arms were there to take her the rest of the way.

And then the Masterson brothers were pulling Pip out of the raging waters. Nate turned Pip on her side and smacked her on the back. Pip expelled lungsful of water.

Phoebe collapsed on the grass and tried to catch her own breath. *Joel.* They needed to find him. Find the Rutherfords before they hurt someone else.

She rolled to her side, coughing, trying to get

the water out of her own lungs. Dirt flew up around her.

Hard hands grabbed her and yanked her behind a large boulder.

She looked up into Matt's green eyes. Green eyes the same as his brother's. *"Stay! He's shooting at you!"*

At least that's what she thought he said. Phoebe wasn't taking any chances, but her *sisters* were exposed.

She yelled their names, wishing she could just *hear* them.

One of the twins was lifted over the boulder and shoved toward her.

Pip. Phoebe wrapped her arms around her little sister.

Matt came behind them. He crowded her and Pip together, then covered them with his own body, trapping them against the rock.

Phoebe just held her sister and clung, praying Joel and Perci and Nate were all going to be *ok*.

39

They'd just about pulled the third Tyler woman from the water when the shots rang out from above. They missed Phoebe by inches, but Nate doubted the woman had realized what it was. He wrapped Persephone in his arms and yanked her behind the large tree. He covered her with his own body, protecting as best he could.

She was still tied to the damned trunk—like a sacrificial goat—as water rushed over them both from the knees down.

Another shot struck far too close to her face for his comfort, sending shards of bark into the air. Nate pulled his knife free and sliced through the rope.

He dragged her toward the rocks sheltering her sisters.

They'd just reached the edge of it when a shout rang out above. Nate looked toward the ledge, just in time to see a large male body fall.

For one long horrific moment, he was terrified he'd just watched his older brother die.

Until someone shouted his name from above.

Joel waved from the top of the ledge then called for Phoebe.

Thank God, it hadn't been his brother.

Nate yelled back.

40

JOEL WAS GOING TO PASS OUT AT ANY MOMENT. He just hoped he'd reach the relatively flat clearing where his brother was before that happened.

Before he closed his eyes, he needed to see for himself that Phoebe was safe.

They met him halfway down the hill.

He hadn't realized Matt and the twins were there, too. But he pushed thoughts of them aside. He just needed to see *her*.

He looked at Nate. "Where is she?"

Nate reached for him and cursed. "Damn it, Joel. She's safe. Perci's seeing to her now. How badly are you hurt?"

"I've been shot. But I need to see Phoebe." He pushed past his brother. Headed toward the two redheads leaning over a third. He said her name, even though he knew she probably couldn't hear him at the moment. He just needed to say it.

He'd thought he'd lost her before they'd even had a chance together. No more. He was going to take his chance, no matter what.

She sensed him or something. Big Tyler blue eyes popped open, and she looked straight at him. *"Joel!"* And then she was reaching for him. "You're *bleeding*. Perci, he's still bleeding! Tom Rutherford shot him."

Nate turned his brother toward him. Joel protested, turned back to the woman struggling to stand.

"Small-caliber rifle." Joel gasped out. He reached for Phoebe with the arm he could still feel. She slipped against his side, and he just held her for a long moment.

She and her sisters were mud soaked, but he'd never seen a trio so beautiful. She'd been in the water, hadn't she? And her sisters had gone in after her.

Apparently so had Matt and Nate, who were soaked themselves.

He had a lot to be thankful for. But first...he looked at his brother. "Is she hurt?"

"*Yes*. We need to get you both to the hospital. But she's better off than you are. At least she's not bleeding anywhere that I know of."

"Take care of her. You take care of my girl *first*, Nate. You promise me that. Matt can patch me up in the meantime. But *you* take care of *her* first."

It was the last thing Joel said.

He pitched forward into his brother's arms as the darkness claimed him.

41

THEY WRAPPED HER IN A WARM BLANKET THEN did the same to Perci and Pip. The three of them sat shivering on the same hospital bed. The state police and someone said *DEA* would be there soon to take their statements. Phoebe had missed most of it.

Tom Rutherford was dead. There was no way he could have survived that fall. No one knew where his brother had ended up. It was just sheer luck that Joel had survived up there. She tried to fight off the shock, but couldn't.

He'd missed falling over that damned forty-foot cliff by *inches*. Inches. That's all it would have been.

And for what? *Marijuana?* A few simple bucks? She'd heard the brothers arguing over *pot* plants before she'd lost her hearing aid when she'd fallen. Pot. On Tyler property.

It had all been about them growing illegal drugs.

Why their ranch? Had it been because he'd wanted to make trouble for their family by getting *Phoenix* into trouble? That's what Matt had said he'd been told. Phoebe could hear again. Pip had had the foresight to grab the spare hearing aid Phoebe kept in her bedside table. It wasn't the best, but she could hear again. She had that again, at least.

Phoenix had apparently awakened a few hours ago and spilled the whole entire story to Pan and Joel's brother Levi.

He'd spotted Rutherford on their property over a week ago. The day after, the bloody message had arrived. Phoenix had followed, found the pot plants Rutherford had planted on the corner of the Tyler property. He'd overheard Rutherford and his brother laughing about how if they were ever caught they'd just blame the Tylers. It had been a sick sort of revenge.

Phoenix had been afraid *Joel* would blame

their family if he saw them like the previous sheriff had blamed Phoenix for the wreck.

Phoenix had tried to bring Rutherford down himself. It hadn't happened.

It had just made things so much worse. Until Rutherford had caught Phoenix snooping and beaten him within an inch of his life.

And then Rutherford had gone to the cabin to find any evidence Phoenix had collected.

He'd found Joel and Phoebe instead.

The shivering wouldn't go away.

Joel had almost died. *She* had almost died.

If it hadn't been for her sisters and his brothers, they both would have.

Pip and Perci shifted closer simultaneously, once again doing that twin thing of knowing what the other was thinking. Phoebe took some comfort in that.

Perci was uncharacteristically quiet. Pip asked Phoebe if she was going to be ok.

Phoebe wasn't certain.

She needed to see Joel.

"I need Joel."

She looked at her sisters and knew they looked just as she did. They looked like they'd been through a literal mud-drenched hell. She wiped at her eyes quickly, and her own hand came away covered with mud.

They needed showers. Why hadn't the hospital let them take *showers?*

They weren't in any danger of dying. Her arm hurt—it might be broken, she wasn't certain. They had walked into this hospital on their own two— ok, six—legs. They would walk out of it on their own legs, too.

But first, she needed a shower. And she needed to make certain *Joel* was ok.

She didn't realize tears were slipping down her cheeks to mingle with the mud until Perci told her not to do that. That it was only going to make the mud on her face worse. Her sisters both reached for the box of tissues on the table.

"We need showers. Let me see what's taking so long." Perci slipped from the hospital bed gingerly.

Phoebe cataloged her movement. Perci had borne the brunt of the pressure, the force of the water raging around her as she'd struggled to keep Pip from being yanked away.

The current could have snapped that rope and swept Pip down the raging river, just as it could have Phoebe if she'd not been lucky enough to grab that tree root.

And it could have swept Perci right out along with them.

They could *all* have died because of a madman's thirst for revenge and his greed.

Had the Masterson brothers not made it to the river at the last minute...Phoebe *couldn't* think about that right now. They had survived, and that madman hadn't. She and her sisters were hurting and bruised, but they were *alive.* And that was all that could matter.

She needed a shower.

And she needed *Joel.*

Not necessarily in that order.

42

Nate looked at the bedraggled young woman standing in the midst of the ER, and something in him cracked. There were more fire and backbone in that woman than *ten* men at times. Today had just cemented that for him.

Never would he forget seeing her standing there hugging a damned *tree,* almost chest-deep in a raging flood, with a rope wrapped around her waist while she held her sisters' safety in her hands. Never would he forget the hope and relief that had been in her eyes when he'd wrapped his arms around her and helped pull her sisters from the waters.

And never would he forget how she looked right now.

"Persephone?"

"We need showers. And Phoebe's going crazy. She needs to know how he is. And soon. I think her arm's broken and she won't let me see again. She just wants to sit there and wait for word on him. *He's* all she can think about. She's going to go into shock soon."

She was shivering and soaked through.

He looked at Tiff, the head nurse on shift. She had a compassionate look on her face, a look he understood. "Tiff, her sisters need showers and dry clothes. Blankets. And talk to Dr. Rodrick; I want him to take a look at Perci's sister Phoebe personally, ok?"

"Sure thing, Dr. Masterson." Tiff held a hand out to the younger woman. "Come on, Perci. Let's get you and your sisters taken care of."

She'd just started down the hall with Perci when the ER doors opened. Nate's youngest brother rushed in, the smallest Tyler clinging to him like a monkey.

Their new housekeeper held the hands of the other two boys.

The rest of the Tyler children had arrived.

Pan's eyes widened, and she cried out when her gaze landed on Perci. "Oh, Perci..."

Perci held up a hand. "It's been one hell of a day, Pan. I'll tell you all about it. *Later*."

Pan held herself together. "I think I'll take you up on that. Where're Phoebe and Pip."

"We're going to take showers. That's all I'm saying now."

"I think that'll be a good idea." Pan just stared. "Hey, Perci?"

"Yeah?"

"We love you, you know? No matter what crazy stunts you pull. Or any of the others. Heck, even what stunts *I* pull. We're Tylers. It's kind of what we do."

Perci smiled. "I know. We're Tylers. Crazy stunts are in our genes. Love you guys, too."

Nate waved her on her way.

They were Tylers. For the first time, he was getting a true inkling of what that meant.

43

ALL NATE HAD BEEN ABLE TO TELL HER WAS that Joel had been taken back to surgery to fix the damage to his collarbone, which had taken a hit from a bullet. He'd insisted his brother was going to damned well be fine, no matter what. Nate's attitude reassured Phoebe. Some. She wouldn't breathe again until she saw him for herself.

She wasn't about to let him see her looking like a grubbling. A mud-coated grubbling at that.

The nurses, all friends of Perci's, pulled together and found her and her sisters some clean clothes to wear. A shower had never felt so good.

She was clean now. And all she had to do was *wait*.

Until Nate got a close look at her.

He lifted her into his strong arms right in front of everyone and carried her from the surgical waiting room back to the ER department, even though she fought to stay near Joel. He put her in a wheelchair and admonished her to sit still or else. He was going to take her to radiology himself.

He muttered under his breath about damned foolish, stubborn Tylers, but his hands were gentle. Worried. Because he cared. What he'd said to her was that he'd promised Joel he'd take care of her.

He wheeled her past the information desk just as her father rushed in. "*Phoebe Kate!* What happened? Where are your sisters?"

"They're taking showers, Daddy. We're ok. We're all ok."

"No one will tell me what in the hell's going on around here. I got a call in Texas saying half my kids were at the hospital. Where's that damned sheriff?"

"Oh, Daddy!" Phoebe lost the battle with tears. There were going to be so many questions, with answers she wasn't certain that *she* had.

How was she supposed to hold herself together?

Her father lifted her from the wheelchair and rocked her while she cried.

44

HIS BROTHER'S GIRL HAD A BROKEN ARM, FIVE cracked ribs, abrasions and contusions too numerous to count, and a mild concussion. The river —not to mention Rutherford's damned fists—had done a real number on her.

It amazed Nate that she was still standing.

Until he realized what she was doing. If she let on how badly she was hurting, she'd be rushed upstairs and treated with pain management drugs. Kept away from the damned surgical department, that was for certain. Kept away from Joel.

Matt stood silently at the door to the smaller private waiting room, doing his best to keep the gawkers out. The word that the sheriff had been injured taking down a major drug operation, as well as what had happened to the Tyler sisters, was starting to get around.

People wanted to look, just to say they had.

Damned despicable how people acted when a disaster of some sort struck their neighbors. At least in Nate's estimation.

The four sisters stuck to the small couch, wrapped in blankets and close to one another. Nate contacted the maintenance technician on duty and had the room's thermostat adjusted behind the security tag. The three eldest needed to be kept warm.

He wasn't used to Perci so quiet or appearing so frail. She was sitting there next to Phoebe and looking half asleep. And shivering.

He'd given orders to the ER staff that she and her twin be thoroughly examined to make sure they hadn't done internal damage. They'd both passed with flying colors on the internal damage but would be extremely sore for several days. They had to be hurting. Perci's hands were abraded from the rope, and her abdomen was bruised from the constant tightening of the rope. Pip had a few cracked ribs from the pressure of the water fighting against the rope that had slipped up under her breasts. One of her arms was raw from being hit by a piece of debris. She had an abrasion over her right eyebrow. She'd no doubt scar, to match her twin once again.

Phoebe looked like a little survivor of war.

All three had stubbornly refused anything stronger than ibuprofen.

Why? Why were Tylers so damned obstinate?

Nate stood. He'd get an update about his brother again. Maybe that would be enough to spur them into taking care of themselves while they waited.

45

LIGHT FROM THE WINDOW TOLD JOEL IT WAS probably pretty early. From the monitors attached to him and the lovely piece of wardrobe covering him, he knew exactly where he was.

What he didn't know was where *she* was. He reached for the call button that he knew would be somewhere nearby.

Nate came in almost immediately. "Damn. Way to cause a scene, big brother. Nice, dramatic finish and everything."

"Where is she?"

"Next door. Resting, I think. She's mighty stubborn and keeps trying to sneak in here with you. Now that you're awake, and the hospital can get your permission, I'll happily lock her in here with you. She's as difficult as any other Tyler—that's for sure."

Joel grinned. "Always knew you had my back. Seriously? The damage?"

"You took a—"

"To *her*." He could feel the damage done to himself. That wasn't what concerned him at all.

"Like that, is it? Thought as much. She'll be ok, Joel. Her arm is broken, and she has some cracked ribs and a concussion. She's exhausted. She still hasn't slept fully, yet. I'm thinking of drugging her into submission. I thought Persephone was the most difficult Tyler on the planet, but *your* girl might just have her beat."

"Nate, quit talking. I want my girl. Be a good little brother and go fetch her for me."

46

PHOEBE LOOKED UP WHEN THE BIG MAN WHO so greatly resembled Joel walked into the room she was currently being held hostage in. He smiled, just as handsome as his brother.

"Joel?"

"He's awake and demanding I fetch you."

Phoebe climbed off the bed quickly, ignoring the aches and pains that she suspected were going to be her companions for a week or so. "Let's go."

"Yes, ma'am. I live to serve."

"Ha ha. No one likes sarcasm. Have you ever heard that before?" She snarked at him, but he'd earned her loyalty over the last several hours. Just seeing how much he'd worried about his brother had done that. And the kind way he'd dealt with her, not to mention with Perci and Pip. He and Perci might not get along very well, but Phoebe had finally gotten his measure.

Nate Masterson was an old softie where the wounded were concerned.

And then she wasn't thinking of his brother at all.

Joel was awake. And reaching for her.

Phoebe just stood there and stared. She didn't even notice when Nate stepped out of the room.

"Honey?" Joel said, almost too softly for her to hear.

She stepped closer until she could touch him. "I thought they were going to kill the both of us. *You*. And I was angry. Because just like with my mother, I didn't get the chance to say the things I wanted to."

"I know. Hell of a beginning, isn't this?"

"Yes."

"Come closer. I'd like to hold you, but they have me on a bunch of damned leashes. I won't tell you where that one goes." He indicated one suspicious tube that went under the blanket.

"Is there room?"

"Honey, you're not all that big. I'll make room." He shifted carefully, creating a small free spot near his feet. "Come here."

Phoebe climbed. "I don't want to hurt you."

"I can deal. I think they have me on some pretty nice meds here." He shifted again, then grimaced. "Wish they had extra-large beds here at this hotel."

The hand not trapped by the IV reached for her. He kept guiding her until he was partially on his uninjured side, and she was on hers, facing him. "There. That's better."

It was. They'd have to be careful—the hospital bed was narrow, and they were both injured—but now they could be there, together.

Exactly where she wanted to be.

"Joel?" She said his name as she snuggled there and just breathed him in.

"Yes, honey?"

"I think I've decided what I want to do about you." Her eyes started to drift closed as the fear running through her went away. He was going to be ok. They both were. They *all* were.

"And what is that?"

"Can I just stay right here next to you forever?"

"I think that will be a damned fine idea, honey." He wrapped his free hand around hers where they rested between them. He held her until they drifted off, together.

EPILOGUE

Nate checked on his brother an hour after he'd let Phoebe out of her own bed. What he found didn't surprise him in the least. Although he would never have thought it possible to get two people in the same hospital bed, they had.

He studied the two for the longest time, thinking that they looked damned good together. Like they belonged exactly where they were.

Someone came in the room behind him, and he turned, not surprised to see dark-auburn hair and the biggest thorn in his side.

"I couldn't find her," Perci said. She came around from Nate's back and got closer to the bed. She looked up at him. "She looks at peace. I can't remember the last time I saw my sister without her looking worried about something. Even in her sleep."

Nate didn't know what to say after that, so he didn't say anything at all. The way his brother was holding that girl...

Nate couldn't help feel a bit of envy. "They're good for each other."

"I guess. I'm just glad they're both here to be good for each other. It was so close..."

Nate looked at her quickly. "*Don't* start crying. Demons don't get to cry."

"*I'm* not the devil, Masterson." She glared at him out of those blue eyes of hers. But this time, there didn't seem to be much heat. "You are. But...I have to admit. You came in handy yesterday. You saved my sister's life. Possibly Pip's, too. I'm never going to forget that. So...thank you."

Nate nodded. "Let's get out of here. Let them have some peace. I think they've *both* earned it."

Nate quietly closed the door behind them. It was time to go on.

WHAT'S NEXT FOR PIP & MATT?

Safety is more than just elusive...

It doesn't exist.

Pip Tyler is safe at her family's ranch, tending her horses, helping raise her younger brothers—and healing from an attack from when she'd been a teenager.

Her self-imposed isolation ends when her older sister marries the sheriff of Masterson County. Now she has to make room in her life for her brother-in-law—and his three brothers.

Bigger, stronger, larger-than-life, the Masterson brothers have her quaking in her boots every time they get near. Pip doesn't know how much longer she can hide.

He sees more than she knows...

But one brother knows.

Dr. Matt Masterson spends his days building the only veterinary practice in Masterson County—and his nights wondering how to break through Pip's fears. How to get close to the woman he can't forget.

He's not the only one who wants her...

Matt isn't the only one who wants Pip Tyler. Someone from her past will stop at nothing to have the woman he's always wanted...as his future.

The only thing standing in his way is the one man Pip knows she can trust...

HER SISTER Phoebe's marriage that afternoon had changed everything about Philippa Tyler's world.

Phoebe had been the center of their family since they'd lost their mother almost two and a half years

ago. She'd handled the day-
to-day running of the Tyler ranch where they had
all lived. Kept them all going through some of the
darkest days of Pip's lives.

And she'd taken over the raising of Pip's
youngest three brothers.

Pete, Parker, and Patton were going to be Pip's
responsibility for a while. Until the Tylers figured
out what to do next. Phoebe's marriage changed
everything. For everyone.

Phoebe and her new husband, the sheriff of
their county, hadn't wanted to wait to marry after
they'd nearly been killed. No one really blamed
them. Pip didn't.

Joel Masterson adored her sister. And had
risked his life to keep her sister safe.

Phoebe being married to one of the county's
most prominent citizens meant the isolation Pip
had always counted on for their family at the Tyler
ranch was no more.

Tonight at the wedding reception she'd been
forced to deal with far too many people for her
sanity. She'd had to escape before she lost the
ability to breathe completely.

For Pip, escape had always meant one place.

The horse barn.

Sky Dancer, the gelding she herself had delivered when she'd been only sixteen, whickered when she entered the stable that would be his new home. Pip greeted him quietly then rubbed against the soft nose. This was one of her babies, and she would miss seeing him every day.

She liked horses far better than she did people. There was no doubt about that in her head. Horses weren't as mean, as malicious, as people. It was as simple as that.

The itch to ride was hard to resist. Pip slipped out of the small jacket that covered her only piece of formal wear, a pale pink dress that was a bit too tight, and far too short. She didn't like dresses much, always feeling exposed and naked in them.

She was more comfortable in flannel and jeans. But for Phoebe, she'd made the effort.

They'd come so close to losing her older sister, just like they'd lost their mother so abruptly.

None of her family took that lightly. If Pip had to step up and fill Phoebe's shoes with the rest of the Tylers, then she would.

She'd just do what she had to do; but tonight... tonight she just needed to get away. To ride. And that was what she did.

Dr. Matt Masterson, the only vet in Masterson County, knew pretty much every horse on the property jointly owned by him and his brothers. And he knew the big bay gelding shooting across the field just as the sun was setting.

He even knew the redhead riding like the wind.

First, the horse was distinctive, and belonged to his brand-new sister-in-law. Second, there were only a handful of redheads quite that small anywhere in Masterson County. Third, there were only four women he'd ever seen ride like that.

One redhead was inside, coordinating the party as his family's housekeeper, the eldest redhead had just been carried away in his brother Joel's arms, and the third had just left to work her shift at the Masterson General Hospital, along with his younger brother Nate.

That left little Pip as the only real possibility.

Pip.

The quiet one. The one who looked at the world with fear. He had yet to figure her out. She was so afraid, especially of men, yet when faced with losing a loved one, she was the bravest woman he had ever seen.

He'd never forget seeing that bravery in action. He still dreamed about that day, about her, in the middle of the night.

Something about the quietest Tyler sister had stayed with him. From the moment he'd dragged her from a raging river and covered her body with his own while a madman tried to kill them all. He'd thought of that woman nightly, at least, ever since.

He stepped up to the fence and just watched as she flew across the field, the animal beneath her. He could almost sense her hurt, her confusion.

Her fear. It was that fear that kept him from acting on the attraction that burned in him—even months after that day.

A luxury sedan slowed on the highway that bordered their pasture, across the field, and Matt suspected he wasn't the only one captivated by the sight of the fairy—every Tyler female looked like a damned fairy—flying across the field on the back of a red unicorn.

She slipped from the back of the horse and began walking him down. Matt made certain to stay in the shadows.

Matt didn't want to frighten her. Pip was so easily frightened.

He had yet to figure out why.

Falling

Hiding

Seeking

FINLEY CREEK SERIES

TRILOGY ONE (TEXAS STATE POLICE)

Her Best Friend's Keeper

Shelter from the Storm

The Price of Silence

TRILOGY TWO (FINLEY CREEK GENERAL)

If the Dark Wins

Wounds That Won't Heal

Hope for Finley Creek (bonus novella)

As the Night Ends

TRILOGY THREE (FINLEY CREEK DISASTER)

Before the Rain Breaks

Lost in the Wind

Walk Through the Fire

MASTERSON COUNTY NOVELLA SERIES

Seeking the Sheriff

Discovering the Doctor

Ruining the Rancher

Denying the Devil

SMALL-TOWN SHERIFFS

Holding the Truth

SUSPENSE/THRILLER

PAVAD: FBI CASE FILES

PAVAD: FBI Case Files #0001

"Knocked Out"

PAVAD: FBI Case Files #0002

"Knocked Down"

PAVAD: FBI Case Files #0003

"Knocked Around"

PAVAD: FBI Case Files #0004

"White Out"

PAVAD: FBI Case Files #0005

"Buried Secrets"

Calle has several free reads available at

www.**CalleJBrookesReads.com**

For my grandfather, the best man I have ever known.

You will be missed.

Oct. 2015

For my grandmother, who gave me the courage to try.
Without you and your love of romance, I never would
have made it this far.

Feb. 2016

For my papaw, whose children loved him deeply, and
will always miss him.

Oct. 2017

Calle J. Brookes enjoys crafting paranormal
romance and romantic suspense. She reads almost
every genre except horror. She spends most of her time
juggling family life and writing while reminding herself
that she can't spend all of her time in the worlds found
within books. CJ loves to be contacted by her readers
via email and at **www.CalleJBrookes.com**. When
not at home writing stories of adventure and wrangling

with two border collies and a beagle puppy, CJ is off in her RV somewhere exploring the beautiful world we live in, along with her husband of she can't remember how many years and their child.

www.ingramcontent.com/pod-product-compliance
Lightning Source LLC
Chambersburg PA
CBHW031328170626
46807CB00002B/612